Acknowledgments

S0-BOF-153

Thank you so much to Paula Gibson, Kira R., and Shona M. for all your help. A lot of time and effort went into this from you guys and I appreciate it.

ONE

GREEN, BROWN, DEAD

July 28

The flesh rotted before the mind as the soul succumbed to death. Dying was the easy part, and even then it wasn't over.

It was a horrible thing to watch someone you love suffer from the virus that ravaged the Earth. It was far worse for the person who contracted it. A simple scratch, bite, or whatever way the virus entered the system caused an instant reaction. The body quickly deteriorated, breaking down physically while fever raged and the sickness became more than any one person could bear, suffering pain, agony, and despair while the skin blackened and swelled, until finally madness took over their mind, transforming the person into an enraged lunatic set on destroying and tearing apart whoever was in their path. Even when the heart stopped beating, when their lungs ceased to take in air, the body kept going. A mindless, soulless body destined to keep attacking.

But were they truly mindless? Did they have a soul?

I often wondered. They were physically dead, their bodies quickly decomposing as they moved. Yet there was something in their eyes, something that showed recognition, even desperation. It was as if when they opened their mouths, the noise they made was actually a cry for help.

'Help me, please, do something. Save me.'

Maybe they knew what they were doing, but just couldn't stop it.

1

We'd never know, unless we became one of them.

I was fighting like hell not to let that happen. So had my father.

His last words to me were, "Come sit with me, Nila, I don't have much time left."

Those words were spoken just before he took his own life. My father was bitten and contracted the virus. The bite he received was not only from an infected, but from his own flesh and blood... my brother.

It was ironic. My brother, the brilliant doctor battling the virus, the one that saved my father's life in a sense, was the one who ended it.

We were fortunate to be given a heads up about the virus from my brother Bobby, who worked for the CDC. He told us to start stockpiling, and we did.

We had everything we needed to survive and at my brother's suggestion we retreated to my father's cabin. All we had to do was wait it out.

The cabin was away from the city, secluded, and surrounded by a fence we doubly reinforced. It was impenetrable by any physical being. However, a virus is not physical. It can seep through a single drop of blood, or unsuspectingly in a small child.

Our camp bordered that of the Big Bear campsite owned by life-long friends. Many had the same idea as we did, run to the hills, get away from civilization, and wait.

Like good neighbors we worked together, doing our best to survive. It wasn't enough. The virus had already invaded, we just didn't know it.

There were hundreds of people between the two campsites in the beginning.

Then one by one everyone died...and many came back.

I lost so much. My husband, my daughter, my father and brother, even my stepmother and a friend.

Those were only the people around me. Outside our fences, outside our mountain, I didn't want to think about how many people I knew that had died.

Nearly everyone on the mountain was gone. Only four of us remained. There was me and my four year old daughter, Katie. Edi Reis, was still with us. She was an eighty year old woman who came to Big Bear with her husband Manny every year. Edi and her husband eventually moved to our property when Big Bear fell. Manny passed away from natural causes. And last, but definitely not least, was Lev Boswick.

I don't know what I would have done without Lev.

I had known him my entire life. We had been friends since he came to America from Serbia at ten years old when he was adopted by the Boswick family who owned Big Bear. He didn't speak a word of English at first, however, that didn't stop us from being best friends. We had our ups and downs later in life. All that was put in the past when the virus hit.

Lev was there for everyone and kept going strong even when his own father died of the virus.

Strong as an ox, with a heart as big as his body, Lev was our rock.

We stayed at my father's cabin for months. We weren't the only ones alive, we couldn't be.

We found out the military had initiated places called Green Areas. Camps placed in towns that were still alive, with low levels of infection. According to maps we found, there were many Green Areas. We didn't know, after all the time that had passed, if they were still operational.

There had also been radio contact with other survivor camps, one in Kansas, another in Kentucky, but those contacts dwindled to nothing. I believed their radios died, and they didn't have a solar generator like we did.

They were out there still alive, like the Green Zones. We just had to find them.

That was my goal, to find life.

Bobby knew the virus well, he had worked on it for months. Eventually it would burn out, and all those infected would cease to exist. We only had to wait it out.

I thought we had waited long enough. It was time to leave our mountain sanctuary and our safe haven cabin to find others. I believed that was what we needed to do.

The cabin was left stocked in case we had to retreat there again. We took what we could in the truck and left to find others.

Our first destination was a Green Area located at a mall in Lancaster, Ohio. It was the closest one. After driving through half a dozen desolate towns, we remained hopeful. After all, we hadn't seen a single infected. That was a good thing. However, we didn't see a single uninfected either.

There had been a Green Area at the mall, but when we got there it was deserted. There wasn't a sound.

Fingers in the chain link of the fence, Lev stared out. "Did you really believe we'd find anything here?"

I walked up to him. "Yes."

"We drove for four hours and saw no one."

"We can't be the only ones left, Lev. We can't."

"Does it matter?" I huffed out a breath of disbelief. "Yes. It does."

"Why are we doing this? Why do we need this?"

"Katie needs more than just us."

"No she doesn't," Lev said. "Maybe in the future, not now. She doesn't need to see this…" he spanned his hand across the scene before us, "… dead world."

"That's right, she needs to see life. We need to find life."

"Don't you get it?" Lev stepped closer. "We are life. You, me, Katie, and Edi. We have life, we don't need to find it."

"If we wait too long, we may never find anyone," I said, shifting my eyes to the camp.

"You think these people moved?" Lev asked. "The longer we're out here, the more chance we have of never finding a soul. What if those who lived are doing what we are doing? Searching? Then we become nothing but wanderers and targets for the desperate."

"What are you saying, Lev?"

"I'm saying I will do whatever it is you want to do. If you want to go to the next place, we will. Kentucky? We'll go there. However, I believe if you are looking for life, we already left it."

"The cabin?"

Lev nodded. "It's the best example of 'Green' you can get. Trees, plants, deer that drive us nuts."

"And graves. That's not life."

"Those aren't graves, those are people we love. A reminder of our lives." He inched closer and lowered his voice to a whisper. "The truth is, I *am* scared. I'm scared that we drove away from our best chance at living."

"You'll do what I want to do?"

Lev nodded.

I wrapped my arms around his waist and embraced him. Closing my eyes, I felt a single tear roll down my face and I stepped back. "Okay."

"Okay?"

"Okay. Let's go back."

"Are you sure?"

I looked at the dead camp then to the truck full of supplies that were only a portion of what we still had back at the cabin. "Yeah, I'm sure."

Lev gave me a forced, closed mouth smile, kissed me on the forehead, and we returned to the truck.

"Are we staying, Mommy?" Katie asked when we got back in.

"No, honey," I said. "We're choosing life."

Lev backed up the truck and we drove away, heading back to our cabin, our home. We would drive back through every single deserted town, and I would wonder the whole way if I made the right decision.

It would take another four hours to return. We'd get there before evening, with maybe some time left to unpack.

There was something off with Lev after we left the Green area. I didn't bring it up, but I would later when Edi and Katie were asleep. I needed to ask him what he saw. I believe he saw something because the whole way back to the cabin he kept checking the rearview mirror. He wouldn't do so in a dead world, unless he was afraid something could possibly follow us.

ONE

FROM LEV'S SIDE

The human race had always been monsters, long before the virus physically transformed them. When I was eight years old, I watched my biological parents and grandmother killed right in the main room of our small house, in front of my eyes. I didn't know how to comprehend the horror of what happened. Maybe it was a blessing I was so young. I can still see my mother looking down at me as I sat on the floor playing with the Legos that the church had given us. She smiled at me, mending my father's work pants. My father was working on something, while my grandmother complained that I was making a mess on the floor.

Our front door flew open, my mother looked up, and no one had time to react.

They shot my father, shot my mother, and slit my grandmother's throat.

I screamed and ran to my mother's body. My arms clung to her and I could feel the blood from her chest soaking into my shirt. I held her, waiting for my turn to be killed. It didn't come. Those militant men, or whatever they were, spared me for some reason. After our home they hit the others in our small town, killing even the children.

I didn't know why. Senseless acts of violence, of war, whatever the reason, I was not included, I was chosen. They ripped me from my mother. I wanted to be brave, not show them that they frightened me. I took a deep breath, kept a locked stare on my mother, and held back the tears.

I would not cry again in my life. At least not when anyone would see it.

The men kept talking about how big I was and would end up getting. I was a big child, heavy too. The other kids would poke fun, because how could I be so thick when my family was so poor and without food?

"Koliko si star, dečko?" they kept asking. "How old are you, boy?"

"Osam," I answered. Eight. It was the only thing I ever said in my short time with them.

They raided a few more times, killing, bringing me along and leaving me in the back of the truck to listen to the screams and cries of fear. Then these same men were brutalized by another band of men, and I was left in a dead town. Bodies everywhere, insects and bugs, animals chewing on the dead, and a stench I never forgot. I wish I was old enough to know why it all happened and could understand it. I didn't even think about where I would go, or how I would live. When you are eight years old, dying isn't part of the equation.

I remained in that small village. In a few days authorities came and found me. They took me to a church and I was placed in three different facilities until finally, and fortunately, I ended up in one just outside of Belgrade.

The workers there were nice, I was quiet, still in shock I suppose over what happened to my family and all that I had been through. The orphanage was volunteer run. I remember one older woman, the 'Baba' of the place, took a special interest in me, constantly giving me extra food and trying to fix my hair, which was always wild and rejected every comb.

"Tako je tužno momak. Jedi. Budi srećan," she'd say and hand me cakes. "Such a sad boy. Eat. Be happy."

She made me happy, and through her I met Barry Boswick, the man who would become my father. I don't, never have, or ever will use the phrase 'adoptive father', because he was more than just someone who adopted me.

It was two years from the time my family was murdered until the adoption was finalized. Although they tried to teach me English before I left, I was linguistically ill prepared. I had a basic understanding of the English language, but hadn't a clue how to speak it.

There I was, ten years old, going to a new country and not knowing the language.

My American parents were wonderful and patient. I knew I would love being with them. Finally, since the loss of my own parents, I saw love and caring when they looked at me. They embraced me often and told me how they felt.

I needed that. I was just a child.

When we arrived home, I was excited to see the city. Even more so the street where I was to live. It was filled with people when we arrived and I found out they were there to greet me. My father was a well liked, good man.

One of the first things he taught me was on nodding and shaking my head.

"When in doubt, Lev," he said, "read the person and nod your head. In this world of hate and rushing around, it's better to be a yes man, because no one else will be."

My first introduction to Nila came at that same party. She was sitting on the porch steps of the house next door. I would learn that Nila loved to sit on the porch. My father sent me over to talk to her.

She held a plate of food on her lap and offered me half of her sandwich.

"My dad said to be your friend," she said. "He said I don't have any and I can't scare you away because you won't understand what I am saying."

I nodded.

"So you don't understand me?" She reached beside her. "I thought ahead." She lifted a notebook. "We can draw pictures if we need to talk. It will be fun."

She wrote down her name. "Nila. My name is Nila."

"Lev."

"See? We won't even need this. Besides, we'll be playing together. Who needs to talk?"

Obviously, I did, because nothing I tried to draw or communicate that first summer worked. Nila misunderstood everything. That was fine, because she was my friend. My one and only friend, and over the course of time, before I was fluent in English, we started to not need to draw. We understood each other.

I hated when we were older and a simple misunderstanding put such a wedge between us, I never gave my all to anyone after that. Yet I truly believed the entire time our friendship separation was not meant to be forever.

It wasn't. Although it took a global catastrophe for both of us to see it. The fences should have mended years earlier, not just when we needed real fences to actually survive.

We only had each other in the world, we had to survive. The world wasn't safe, I knew that, and unlike what we had believed when we left the cabin in search of others, the threat to bring mankind to extinction wasn't over. Not by a long shot.

TWO

RETREAT

July 28

The heat was unbearable, and the first thing Edi did as soon as Lev unloaded the solar generator was turn on the back room air conditioner, grab Katie, and claim the small bedroom.

She reminded me that the elderly and young were especially susceptible to heatstroke. I was fine with her doing that. It gave me and Lev a chance to unload the truck.

He was acting strange. Well, strange for Lev. My big friend of few words not only wasn't talking, out of character for him, he wasn't listening either.

He wanted to unload the truck. I wanted to help.

"Put it away as I bring it in," Lev said.

He brought the boxes in, and then he lifted the floorboard hatches. My father had built three large storage spaces under the floorboards, one in the sitting room, one in the large bedroom, and the third in the kitchen.

Lev opened them all. "Keep three days' supply out. No more," he said. "Put as much as you can in the floor storage. Once that is full, we'll secure the shed."

"We had a lot stacked against the walls," I replied. "Is there a reason we're hiding it now?"

"Not hiding, storing. We had a lot more people then. We also weren't going to be here long term. Now we are. I don't want clutter."

"Okay." I said, then asked, "Do we have to do it all right now? Maybe we—"

"Yes, now."

"Wow. Okay." Despite what he told me I knew something was wrong.

Lev was usually a calm, patient man, yet he seemed to be irritated with how slowly I was moving. I didn't get it. He unpacked the radio stuff and brought it to the back bedroom.

"Starting tomorrow I want to call out hourly, try to reach someone, including Helena and Hal. Even if we stay here, we need to find out what is going on out in the world."

What was going on with Lev? Barking out orders, planning ahead, wanting me to try to reach the camps of Helena and Hal when we hadn't heard from them in weeks.

Something was off. I stopped asking questions and did what he requested. A part of me thought maybe he wanted to get settled and get back into the swing of things.

Before we left the cabin to seek out the Green areas and life off the mountain, we had been resolved As resolved as we could be with what we knew.

Six of us arrived at my father's cabin. My husband Paul was the first to die. He was bitten, and by the time we got to safety, he was already infected. It was hard to believe that over the course of nearly four months, fifteen people sought sanctuary on my father's property.

One by one…we became just a few.

Behind the shed were eight graves. My husband, my daughter Addy, my father, my stepmother Lisa, my brother Bobby, a little girl named Hannah, Edi's husband Manny, and our friend Brian Cade.

There were a father and son from Big Bear Camp that had stayed with us, Bill and Bill Junior. They had left to find family and other people. I wondered if they did, or if they fell victim to the world.

Dozens of healthy people fled Big Bear near the end. Where were they now?

My father was the last to pass away. After his death, a few of the infected made their way to our fence. We dispatched them, and it was mainly quiet now.

We were settled. In Lev, Edi's, and even Katie's eyes the cabin was home, and for the long haul. Not me, I needed to see what was beyond our fence. Maybe there was a world out there and we were missing it. In the back of my mind I held hopes that we were merely a small pocket of civilization affected by the virus.

We had heard that Canada wasn't even hit. How would we ever know for sure if we never left our secure, fenced in property?

After dinner and not long after dark, Lev finished unpacking and worked on checking the fences.

I cleaned up, tucked Katie into bed, then grabbed my folders to work on my project. Some would call it silly, but I believed my project was important because it was the history of the end. My cell phone, a piece of technology many believed useless, was my tool. I couldn't make calls, but I took pictures. The cabin, Big Bear, my garden, people... infected. I loaded them on my laptop and Lev had brought the printer and paper from Big Bear and we printed them until we ran out of ink and paper. There were enough printed for me to work on the project though. The photos were part one. Part two was writing down information about each picture and as much as I could recall about them.

In my mind, someone in the future would view them as pages in a history book. I know if I were living in the future, I would want to know as much as I could about what nearly wiped us out.

Perhaps it already *had* wiped us out, and we just didn't know it yet.

The hot day had cooled some and I took the folder and some bourbon out to the porch to work by the light of a lantern. The bourbon was courtesy of my stepmother Lisa, a functioning alcoholic who'd brought enough booze for years. I needed a drink, it had been a long day. I brought two glasses in case Lev ever stopped working.

The porch was peaceful. It had been my entire life. My father had built a huge porch for the cabin and I had been a porch sitter, no matter where I was. I always loved sitting on the steps and not the gliders and chairs. The cabin porch had lots of great memories and sadly, horrible ones as well now.

I shot my own brother on that porch after he attacked and killed Cade.

Cade had been an accidental addition to our cabin family. He was smart, medically knowledgeable, and a friend. He bled out in Lev's arms. His blood still stained the porch.

Every time I stepped on the porch, I saw the bloodstain. Ironically, when I opened my folder, Cade's picture was right on top. It made me smile. It was taken in Evans City when he and I were trapped in a car surrounded by infected after having gone looking for medical supplies. Cade had been bitten and we thought he was going to die. His remarkably good spirits were the result of not only a ton of medical marijuana but the fact that, as we found out later, he wasn't infected.

He took a selfie of us, called it our first and last picture together ever. I grabbed my pen and started writing under the printed picture. I wrote the date, why the picture was taken, and the events before and after.

"Good to see you working on that," Lev said.

I peered up. "You speak."

"I have since I was three." He sat down next to me. "Soon I will go to the Cranberry Walmart and see if I can get another cartridge for the printer."

"I'm still taking pictures."

"I know."

"You're mad."

"I am not mad. Busy. We should have never left in the first place. There was a lot to unpack."

"So why unpack in one day?"

"I wanted to get settled. I wanted to know for sure we had stopped."

I placed my folder to the side, picked up the bottle of bourbon, and poured him some. "You're pissed about leaving." I handed him the glass. "You didn't eat dinner. By the way, Edi is upset about that. You mope, you want to say 'I told you so' to me, you checked the fences ten times. Usually you are polite. You aren't today. Something snapped. You haven't been this annoyed with me since that night when you fought with me about driving when drinking."

Lev's mouth dropped open. "Where is all this coming from?"

"The fact that you barely spoke to me after we left Lancaster, and then only to bark out orders. Obviously you're mad."

"I am not mad."

"Oh, yeah? Well I know you are. When you're mad your dialect slips through."

"My dialect?"

"Yeah, you know, that hint of Russian."

"That's accent, not dialect."

"Same thing."

"No, it is not. Dialect is words, Accent is sound. Then again, you said Russian, I am Serbian. And do not say same difference." He sipped his drink. "Besides, I do not have an accent."

"Lev," I laughed, "you do. As evidenced by the fact that you don't use contractions when you're emotional or mad, which brings out your...." I raised my eyebrow, "...accent."

Lev sighed heavily and loudly, rolling his glass between his hands. "You're right."

"Ah! You said, 'you're' and not, 'you are'. So that means you're not mad anymore."

"I was never mad."

"Okay, then what is it?"

"It's not anger. I was staying focused because I was concerned. Felt guilty maybe. Yeah...guilty. That's it."

"Guilty? Lev, why on Earth do you feel guilty?"

He stared out at the fence, sipped his drink again. "Let's play a word association game."

I cocked back. Did he just switch the subject?

"Word association?"

He nodded.

I sighed. "Fine. Okay, you don't want to talk about it. I get it. Go on."

"Maybe some things are hard to come out and say. Word association."

"Shoot," I said.

"Was that a word for me?" Lev asked. "Because I was going to give you words."

"Lev, I was only saying that for you to go on."

"You don't remember do you?" he asked. "Word association?"

It took a second and then I did. When he and I were kids and his English was really bad, we communicated with word association. As we got older it was our way to talk about things without talking about them. "Oh, wow, yeah. Go on."

"Camp," he said.

"Tent."

"Hide."

"Seek."

He looked at me as if he didn't approve of my response. "Infected."

"Corkers."

Lev nodded. "Station wagon."

"Family."

Silence. He stared out. I could see something was going on behind his eyes.

"So let me see if I can connect the dots. When we arrived at the Green Area, when we were by the fence you saw infected."

"After you said we would come back here you hugged me. I saw them. I hid that from you."

"That's fine. I'm glad you didn't tell me. I don't want to hear about them."

"The infected are still out there," Lev said.

"I didn't think they wouldn't be. Just because we didn't see any on the way didn't mean they were gone. Bobby said less populated areas would be the last to die out. Honestly, I don't get why this caused such a mood, or why it made you feel guilty."

"You are missing a word," Lev said.

I thought about it. "Station wagon. You mean two words."

"Yes."

"I figured it was us."

"No. When we were getting back in the truck I saw a man making a mad dash to close the back door of a station wagon. I could see as we pulled away he was waving for us to stop." He dropped his head. "I didn't."

"Station wagon? You think he had a family?"

"I think he went there like us and...I kept going."

"Why do you feel guilty?"

"For not saying anything, but mainly for leaving. What if he needed help?"

"Would it help if I told you that you're not a big humanitarian outside of the people you care about? I remember one time you saying just that."

"I know."

"So why the guilt?"

"You wanted to find life."

"I did. I'm a little upset that you didn't mention it. I can also see that you knew I'd make you turn around."

"Turning around would have put you, Edi, and Katie in danger. I saw the infected."

I nodded. "Then I understand. Is that why you kept looking in the rearview mirror? You were watching for infected?"

"No," he said. "I was hoping the station wagon followed us."

Hearing him say that shocked me. I refreshed my drink. "Wow. I did not expect you to say were hoping they followed us. Fearful they might have followed us maybe, but not hoping. Lev, it's okay."

"No, it's not."

"Alright, then what can we do about it? What do you *want* to do about it?'

"A part of me wants to head back and look."

"Then do it."

He turned his head toward me. I could see the seriousness and pain in his eyes. He was really affected by that split second decision to leave and say nothing.

"Do it. We'll be fine here, you'll be fine out there. Take enough gas and go. You shouldn't be gone that long."

Lev stared at me. He didn't say what he would, or wouldn't, do. I was sincere with my suggestion. I knew my friend; he was having a hard time with the choice he made, and he needed to make it right. I also knew whatever he decided to do, he needed to know I stood by him and his decision.

THREE

COOP

July 29

In the morning, right after breakfast, Lev told me he needed to go look. I understood that. Although, for a man who had stood his ground about not leaving, he was torn. Knowing him as I did, I imagined his guilt was getting the best of him, just like it did with his friend in New York when the outbreak first occurred. He said he made a lot of self promises after leaving his infected friend. Lev never told me what all those promises were.

I knew Lev. He probably mulled over that station wagon all night, thinking about those who were inside, a family maybe.

He was a do-gooder, he helped people, and he had to try to right a wrong. Whether it would work remained to be seen. At least part of his conscience would be clear. However, if he discovered he could have prevented something horrible by simply turning around, it was something he'd carry the rest of his life.

He didn't have it in him to let it go, or not feel anything about it.

Good people with good hearts don't flip a page in the coldhearted book of life.

I bid him farewell with an embrace and a wish of good luck. Edi prayed for him. I suppose that would help more than my wishing him well.

He packed some gas and took the small generator and hose with him. He'd replenish those cans, he said. That wasn't important. Him having enough gas to get back was.

He had supplies and was armed. I was positive Lev would be fine. He'd be back eventually. I doubted it was going to be in ten hours like he predicted when he left, especially when he said he wanted to check a lot of places around us.

I appreciated his confidence in my ability to keep the camp safe. Other than my being a better shot, we had those fences. They were strong, reinforced, topped off with barbed wire, and decorated with those spikes my father wanted.

Whether they were in their strong or weak phase, the infected weren't getting in. Unless hundreds showed up, I felt safe.

Since the onset I had waited and worried about a horde of them destroying our fence.

They hadn't come…yet. With my luck, they'd show up when Lev was gone. The plan if we were ever surrounded was to break through the back fence and take Rutgers Four Wheel Trail down to the main road. But Lev was taking the truck, so that option wasn't there. We couldn't very well blast out of here in the pop up camper.

I told him if a massive amount arrived at the fence and surrounded us while he was gone, we'd retreat to the storage under the cabin and he'd just have to figure out a way to get us.

After he drove off, I stood at the gate until I couldn't see the truck any longer. I secured the locks and headed back into the cabin to clean up.

I wanted to do it, but Edi insisted, so I ended up helping her.

Katie was back to working on the mural, a pictorial history of events. Addy had drawn on the mural many times. It saddened me to see her images. I missed her terribly and I still blamed myself for her infection. I wasn't thinking. I knew better. I knew an infected didn't always show symptoms right away. Yet when I saw little Hannah, I didn't see a sick girl, I saw a child who needed help. I'd brought her into our family fold, and she infected my daughter.

Even though all that was in the past, the pain would never be go away. It would remain with me and hurt with every breath I took and every time I thought of my child.

Maybe down the road the pain would lessen. More than likely I would simply get used to it.

We didn't speak much following Lev's departure. Edi was a little upset that he had left. She didn't say anything. I sensed it.

After doing the breakfast dishes, she told Katie, "Finish up. You can help me feed the chickens."

"You don't need to occupy her," I said.

"I need the help," Edi replied. "You should rest. You haven't slept."

"Maybe I'll take a nap."

"Good." She held her hand out to Katie. "Let's go feed the chickens."

I remember when Cade heard about the chickens. He poked fun at the ridiculous notion that two eighty year old people were running around with chickens in their pop up camper. I had to tell him that it was only to bring them from Big Bear to our camp. The Reis couple took great care of their chickens. The camper stayed up at Big Bear with a coop built by Manny. They transported the chickens in cages in the back of their truck every season. I swear those chickens were like their children.

Manny and Edi always had chickens for as long as I could remember. Last I knew they had eight. I wondered what happened to them, though I'd never asked. The two chickens on my property now gave us eggs, which I was grateful for.

Lev built a small hen house for them. It wasn't much, but it worked.

He had only been gone an hour and I couldn't get him off my mind. Despite my friend's survivability, I was worried about him. He was out there alone, no one had his back. Every chance I had during the day, I looked around for him.

Before and after my nap, I peered out the window. Then I sat on the porch worked on my project, walked to the gate to look. Ate lunch…walked to the gate, again. Played around with the radios…checked the gate, no Lev.

The hours flew by and when night came and Lev didn't, I was worried even more. Lev gave me a timeframe of ten hours. I always knew he wouldn't be back in that time, so it was no surprise he wasn't there by bedtime. However, that didn't stop my concern.

He'd be back, I knew that, most of all I felt it in my gut. I just didn't know when.

THREE

FROM LEV'S SIDE

With the exception of a couple of teenage years, Nila spent most of her entire life erring on the side of caution. It surprised me when she wanted to leave the cabin to look for survivors. From childhood on, she was always taking the path of least resistance. Although I had not spoken to her in adulthood, I knew what was going on with her life through uninvited commentary from my father.

"I saw Nila today."

"That's good."

"She was wearing an engagement ring. I think she's gonna marry that Paul guy, you know the one who works at Granger Market?"

"Why are you telling me this?" I'd ask.

"I thought you'd want to know."

I didn't want to know. It hurt to know what she did and how I wasn't a part of her life. When she checked out of our friendship, it broke my heart.

Through conversations with my father it was reiterated that as an adult she didn't take risks. The death of her mother strengthened her passive conviction.

However, Nila was strong. She was strong enough to be a mother bear and protect the cabin while I went out to make up for a mistake.

Why didn't I just stop? Why didn't I look at that man standing by the station wagon and wave him over? It was not only a matter of trust but honestly, it was a matter of keeping a tight nest. For a brief moment, I figured the fewer of us there were, the better chance we had at survival. The less chance of me getting close to someone and having them die.

I started life with death. I was sick of it. Not a good attitude to have in a world filled with the dead.

My plan was simple. I was to check the area around our camp, then head out to the Green Area in Ohio. The truck would use up most of our gas supply. I could get more using the generator and pump. I planned on that, even told Nila I would refill what I used.

I hated leaving, but I hated more the fact that I didn't know what became of that man and his station wagon.

I left early in the day and headed up to Big Bear after checking the area around the cabin. It was clear, and I expected Big Bear to be as well, which it was. I went for my bike too. It would use far less gas and get me around a lot easier.

Nila hated motorcycles, never saw the point of them. I'm not sure she ever got over that hatred.

With the world the way it was, riding solo on a bike made a heck of a lot more sense than taking the truck. If I did find someone or more people than I could help on my bike, I'd get them safe and return with the truck. I wasn't going that far from our circle.

I knew I had told Nila I would be gone a half a day, but I wanted to go into the city as well. I wanted to see it. With the barricades, getting through in a truck was impossible.

After checking the immediate surroundings and Big Bear, I would go west to the Ohio Green Area.

The return trip there went smoothly, just like the day before. No one on the road, no infected. Once I got to Lancaster, those few infected I'd seen had turned into hundreds, wandering aimlessly beyond the fence until they spotted me.

The station wagon was gone and they had left the gate open. That told me they escaped and made their way out safely, or at least I hoped that.

It didn't take long for the infected to head my way, and while they were still alive, unfazed by pain or illness, they moved rapidly.

I sped off.

They followed.

At least I saw that the station wagon had gotten away, making me feel somewhat better. I started to head back to the cabin, but it was getting dark. After finding some gas, I stayed in room twelve of a roadside motel, listening to corkers roaming the street, trying to catch my scent.

In the morning I'd head out. I figured north, try to see what was up there, and if it was still light, maybe down to Pittsburgh. I wanted to see what was left of a major city. A part of me kind of wanted to wait. As demented as it sounded, it was something I really wanted to share with Nila.

FOUR

ALL GREEK

July 30

"Do you think Pap is watching us?" Katie asked me. We were sitting on the porch, her with a coloring book, me sharpening another spike. After all, there was no such thing as having too many.

"I think so," I said. "Probably complaining. You know how Pap gets."

"What about Daddy?'

I looked over at her and ran my hand down her face. "I think your father and Addy are too busy being together to look down here. They're leaving that for Pap and Lisa."

"We're easy to spot," she said brightly. "No one is around."

"That's the truth." I peered back to the spike I was making when a breeze swept in. I wouldn't have thought much of it, but it carried a stench. A foul stench of death that caused me to stand up.

"Mommy?"

"Honey, go inside with Edi."

"What is it?"

Shaking my head I stared out toward the fence. I didn't see anything, but I could smell it. I took her arm and led her in the cabin, then I went to the back room and retrieved a rifle.

Edi saw me. "What is it?"

"Nothing that I saw," I said. "I could smell it. It was in the air."

"The Nekros?"

We all had given them names. Infected, crazy, corker—I always liked what Edi called them. The ones infected and enraged she called the Lyssa; those who turned and were dead she called Nekros.

Lev explained that they were Greek names. Nekros, well that was easy; Lyssa was the god of rage. Edi's mother was Greek and she spoke the language fluently.

I took the rifle and went outside. I walked slowly around the perimeter of the fence, looking out, smelling for it. It may have been a while since one approached our fence, but the scent was undeniable.

Nothing was out there that I could see and I walked around twice. The second time around, I paused by the graves in our own cemetery. I hoped we'd never have to dig another hole in the ground while we were at the cabin.

Just as I came around to the front of the cabin, I spotted movement in the distance from the eastern corner of the fence. I poked my head in the cabin, told Edi to stay put with Katie, and I closed the door and engaged the rifle.

Thoughts raced through my mind. What if it wasn't an infected? What if it was a looter or marauder coming toward us? If they had a weapon, I was a walking target.

It was that thought that made me paranoid and I stepped back and went into the cabin.

"Was it nothing?" Edi asked.

"I don't know." I quickly closed all the first floor indoor storm shutters and latched them. The cabin went dark.

"Nila?" Edi questioned, turning on a lantern. "Should I turn this off?"

"No, it's fine. I want to look from upstairs," I said.

What was the matter with me? I was so brave, yet instantly I lost my proverbial balls? I climbed up the ladder steps to the second floor loft and positioned myself by the window.

I stared out for a few minutes and then I spotted it.

It moved quickly and jaggedly through the brush as if looking for something. I could tell by the way it held its arms it was infected.

Infected, not dead.

We had believed that phase of the infection was done, that all that remained were the dead and it was only a matter of time before they rotted and were no longer a threat.

Hal, one of my radio contacts, always said all it would take was one bite and everything reset. Really, all it would take was a group of healthy survivors moving north. One infection. That was it. Damn it.

Back down the ladder from the loft, I walked straight to the door and opened it.

My eyes focused on that corner of the fence, I lifted my rifle as I walked that way. I thought of calling out, drawing its attention, but I opted against that in case there were more out there lurking. I'd rather deal with one at a time. Certainly the blast of the rifle would be enough to call them in.

As I neared the fence, the infected male raced out from the brush running full force at the fence. Enraged infected lacked intelligence. He was so focused on me that he failed to realize not only was the fence in his way, but also those spikes my father placed there.

One impaled him straight through the gut. It didn't kill him, it didn't stop him, it merely held him in place. His legs still moved and kicked as if he were running. His fingers locked into the links of the fence and he made a crackling snarl while his jaw snapped at the air.

His neck was black and the necrosis had created a black spider web on his face. His mouth was covered in fresh blood and it mixed with clumps of hair or fur on his chin. If I didn't know better, I would swear he had something in his mouth. His eyes still had color.

I was about to shoot him when I got a good look and moved closer. I knew him. Yes, his face was pale, his hair matted with blood, but I knew who he was.

Not long ago he and his son had camped on our property, then left to find family. His name was Bill. He obviously never found what he was looking for.

I wondered what happened to his young son, a boy probably nine or ten years old. Was he out there somewhere, or had he met the same fate as his father?

In his infected state, Bill may not have thought about those spikes, but I wondered if he thought about our camp. Had he returned on purpose? Sought us out? Had he met his demise not far from our property? How was that possible? Bill and his son had left weeks earlier. Was it instinct or pure coincidence that he returned?

I knew one thing for sure; Bill wasn't dead. He moved too fast. His legs were still in one piece. The limbs were the part of them that went first from when they tried to walk while decomposing.

He wasn't dead, therefore that smell wasn't coming from him. The odor was still out there, wafting in with each blow of the wind.

It came from the east, from Big Bear.

Our properties were connected. I looked up to the hill. The last time we were up there were no infected around, so when did they return? It was also likely that the smell came from a dead animal, possibly the one Bill had been enjoying.

By the time I stopped skimming the landscape and realized Bill was still snarling away, he had lost a lot of his blood. A huge pool had formed at his feet. He was already pale, and his face was drained of all color now. Bill was still moving and fought to get to me.

It was time to end his suffering. It wasn't fair or humane to let him be like that any longer.

I lifted the rifle and fired a single shot. If there was something in those woods, it wouldn't take long for it to emerge.

FIVE

FANTASY

I waited an hour, standing in that spot, ten feet from Bill, his body still impaled by the spike, slumped inward toward the fence. I waited for more to emerge. None did, although the smell remained.

Maybe it was an animal after all.

I went back into the cabin, told Edi that it was okay to open the shutters, then I sought out a shovel. I wasn't going to bury Bill, I just wanted to push him from the fence. After doing that, I retrieved a cup of lime from the outhouse and, covering my mouth, I tossed it his way.

Surely, a cup wasn't going to do much, but it was all I was willing to spare.

My mind drifted into dark fantasies during the hour I waited and the several hours that followed.

Bill made his way back, just like my brother Bobby made his way to the cabin even in an infected state.

I started to worry and panic. What if Lev was dead? What if he was infected and history repeated with his arrival? Would I be able to shoot him? Would that tiny bit of remaining memory in his head give him the edge to break in?

An infected Lev was a scary thought.

I tried to push those thoughts out of my head, but it was tough. Lev had been gone a day and a half, and my confidence was dwindling fast.

I cleaned up, went inside for lunch, and shared my fears with Edi. That was a mistake, because Katie was full of questions.

"Will he try to eat us? Will he attack us? Lev is strong. Can we fight him?"

I tried to calm her while changing the subject. "I will shoot Lev if I have to. Now what are we working on?"

"In the head?" she persisted. "Pap said when they're dead that's the only way to do it."

"Yes, in the head," I told her. "Now what are you coloring?"

Katie snickered.

"What's funny?"

"Lev in the head. It rhymes."

My eyes widened.

Edi shook her head. "There is a dark side to this child. Who does she get it from?"

"I don't know."

She tilted her head and looked at me hard. "Are you serious?"

The moment she did that, I heard the double beep of a car horn. Rushing to the window, I looked out, exhaled excitedly and grinned. "Lev's back!"

"Oh, good," Edi said. "Now you don't have to shoot him in the head."

I flung open the door and ran to the gate. He was back, he wasn't dead, or infected. Infected didn't drive.

Or did they?

Bobby drove all the way to the property. I stopped before opening the gate.

Lev opened the truck door. "Nila, what are you doing?"

I snapped out of it. "Oh, sorry, nothing, I was lost in thought."

"As you open the gate you get lost in thought?" He got back in the truck, I unlocked the gate, and he drove through, stopping a few feet from me.

I was securing the locks when he walked up to me. I stopped to embrace him tightly. "I am so glad you're back and you're alright."

"Me too." He stepped back. "What's that smell?"

"I don't know what it was before, but now I think it's Bill."

"Bill?"

I pointed.

Lev walked toward the corner of the fence and I finished locking the gate.

"Really, Lev? *Really?*" I trailed him like a puppy dog. He had been back all of ten seconds, and as soon as he saw Bill, Lev had gone out beyond the fence and into the woods for about fifteen minutes. He said he was looking for more infected, specifically for Bill's son, but found none. He reported the smell came from a rotting deer, then dragged Bill's body into our camp.

After bringing him by the shed he retrieved the shovel I had left by the fence.

"Nila, I don't understand what the problem is."

"I want to talk to you," I said. "I want to know what happened. What you saw, didn't see. You were gone two days."

"I had to find fuel and the roads were too dark to move at night."

"Okay…"

"Nila." Lev put the shovel into the ground. "Can we talk after? I'll clean up and we'll sit. This won't take long, I promise."

"Why are you burying him in here?"

Lev paused. "What other solution do you have?"

"You could have dragged him farther into the woods."

"And put him next to the deer?"

"Yes."

"If you think it's bad with the smell of that deer, it would be worse with Bill. I got news for you, Nila." He started digging. "Sprinkling him with the lime didn't work."

"It was the thought that counts."

Lev grunted at me. "It's wrong to leave him out there. We bury him in here. He's a human being and he was one of us."

"For like ten seconds."

"Nila," Lev snapped, "what is wrong with you?"

I stopped for a second and took a breath. "You're right, I'm wrong. I don't know, I'm just...Lev, did you think about this for a second?"

"What? Burying him? Yes. I'm doing it right here."

"No, I mean... Bill left here weeks ago."

"He still deserves to be buried."

"That's not what I mean. He left here weeks ago, yet he came back? Doesn't that concern you?"

"He probably ran into trouble and was on his way when he got infected."

"Exactly. That makes it scarier."

"How so?"

"Because he left a long time ago. Long enough to make it a fair distance. He got infected and like Bobby, still managed to return. Not only do I wonder how," I said, "...but why?"

SIX

BIG STARE

I knew Lev well enough to know there was something he wasn't telling me. Before we had left the cabin for a short run we spent the days doing upkeep on the cabin, farming, and canning. Lev would fish or hunt, I'd sit with Katie teaching her, playing, doing something. Our evenings were mostly clean up, some sort of activity with Katie, then he and I would talk or get into a game of chess if neither of us were in the mood to have a conversation.

Lev seemed as if he was avoiding me. He was staying oddly busy. He peeled potatoes so he could soak them for breakfast. Who willingly peels potatoes? He was avoiding one on one time with me. That alone told me there was something he didn't want to share, because simply, Lev couldn't lie.

He tried. Anytime in our youth he avoided the truth, danced around it, or tried to lie, he'd start breaking into a foreign language. It was odd.

After he dug a grave for Bill, we buried him and had our normal service. Lev told me he wanted to clean up and then we'd talk. That never happened.

Finally, after one excuse or another, I grabbed my project. After kissing Katie, who was oddly being read a story by Lev, I went to the porch.

About a half an hour later, Lev came out to join me. Exhaling heavily he plopped down next to me, causing the board to bounce slightly.

"So," he said. "I hear you wanted to shoot me in the head."

I finished writing my sentence then looked at him. "I take it Katie filled you in."

"She did."

"Well, did she tell you I planned on shooting you only if you returned as one of those things?"

"Yes. Did you think I would?"

I stared out before answering. "No. I knew you would come back, but it was in the back of my mind. Bobby was on his way here, he turned and walked right up to the gate."

"So you thought I would do the same thing?"

"I wasn't ruling it out."

"Do you really think the infected are...thinking?"

I shut the folder. "You tell me."

"I don't know."

"Well neither do I. Not for sure. A part of me believes they are retaining something. Whether that stays after the body dies is a mystery at this point."

"One that will always be."

"What? A mystery?" I shook my head. "You know, Bobby told us an awful lot about this virus. We learned about the infection by living it. We learned about the process of the body by observing pool man. We learned about the decay, the death...but we didn't test him, did we?"

"Test him? You mean to see if he remembered?"

"That, and how long he could survive."

38

"We watched him succumb."

"Under captive circumstances," I said. "I've been thinking about this. You chained pool man and left him to die. How long does it take a human body to succumb without food and water?"

"These things don't eat or drink."

"When they are under medical care. What about when they're out there?" I said. "Maybe it didn't reset, maybe they just found a way to survive longer. After all, Bill was infected. He wasn't dead yet."

"Nila, there's no way Bill was infected for weeks. We have seen what the infection can do. Days maybe...weeks no."

"It could have mutated. That's possible."

"It is. Again, we will never know."

"Yeah, you're right." I sighed and opened my project folder. "Like I never will find out what you were up to and what you saw."

He laughed softly.

"What?" I asked.

"What do you think I saw?"

"I don't know. Bad guys."

He couldn't contain it, his lips fluttered before he laughed. "Bad guys?"

"Yeah, you know, like *Mad Max* type of guys with guns, they rape, they loot. I thought Bill could be one. In fact, that crossed my mind for a split second, and I got paranoid."

"That bad guys were in the woods?"

I nodded.

"I assure you, Nila, there are no bad guys in the woods. I saw no bad guys on the road. Are there bad guys out there? Sure, I suppose there are. I'd like to give humanity a little more credit and think that we're all on the same side here. The infected are bad guys enough."

"We just switched for a moment there."

"What do you mean?" he asked.

"Usually I give everyone the benefit of the doubt. I think of humanity first. I got pretty paranoid yesterday."

In an arrogant manner, which of course was Lev pretending, he sniffed and tilted his head. "Yes, well, that's because I wasn't here. You need me."

"Really?"

"Yes."

"Hmm." I looked down at my folder. "Need you? Nah, I can handle this. However, I suppose I like having you around, but don't let it go to your head."

"It won't."

"So what did you see?"

"Nothing."

"Did you make it back to the Green?"

"I did, and a lot faster since I didn't have to stop for bathroom breaks all the time. And I went to Big Bear and got my bike."

"You *peddled* to the Green?"

"Not a bicycle."

"Aw, Lev," I whined. "You left the truck and rode a motorcycle?"

"Yes."

"I hate them. Why would you take such a risk?"

"I'm fine. I knew you would bitch, that was why I didn't tell you," he said. "The bike got me to the Green pretty fast."

"Did you see the station wagon?" I asked.

"It was gone."

"That's a good thing, right? If they were attacked the wagon would be there. What about the infected you saw in the camp?"

A pause. "Gone."

"They moved on?" Lev nodded. "Then I went to search for gas and took a good look at a few of the towns. Stores were picked through, which tells me there are survivors out there. Then I went north of here, nearly to Erie."

"Cade tried that."

"In the thick of things. There were infected and corkers, all roaming and moving. I didn't see any survivors, but it was clear someone was alive, because some of infected were killed recently. And there is a wall and fence outside the city. People who lived there and left wrote notes. I looked for one from Cade."

"Anything?"

Lev shook his head. "He probably didn't make it that far. I wanted to go see Pittsburgh."

"And?"

"I figured it should be something you and I do together."

"Aren't you romantic?"

He chuckled. "I try."

"What are we doing then, Lev?" I asked. "You used the argument that we come back here, you made it sound like it was dangerous out there. Not only because of the infected, but also regular people."

"We're staying alive here, Nila. Infected are out there and dangerous. People will be too. I am optimistic that there are no *Mad Max* wannabes, but I won't take a chance on that. We stay put, we stay alive."

"They say movement is life," I said.

"Who says that?" Lev asked.

"I heard it once."

"Where?"

"In...in a movie. Brad Pitt or someone said it, I think. Yeah. It sounded solid."

"You're taking words of wisdom on survival from Brad Pitt? It was a movie, Nila, this is real life. We stay for a little while, start preparing for winter. We have to store food and prepare the well."

"This place has survived many winters. It will survive this one too." I closed my folder. "I'm not getting any work done. I'm tired. All this paranoia is wearing me down. Do you mind if I turn in early? I'll relieve you on watch later."

"That's fine."

I stood, leaned over, and kissed Lev on the cheek. "'Night, Lev."

"'Night, Nila."

I headed to the door.

"Nila?"

I stopped.

"No more thoughts of shooting me in the head."

"I'll try. I make no promises." I winked and went inside. It was one of those nights that I felt tired, but as soon as I got in bed, I was wide awake. That didn't last long. Somewhere in the middle of writing, I fell asleep. I was surprised I had held on that long, I had barely slept when Lev was gone. I woke up with my hand still holding the pen. The alarm didn't ring, and the battery had died in the lantern. It was light out and I sprang up. I had failed Lev and slept all night. Then I noticed Katie wasn't in bed, and I figured she had turned off the alarm and lantern.

It was still early. I looked at the wind up alarm clock; it was twenty minutes past six. I slept an hour longer than I wanted to. Poor Lev had been up all night.

The smell of coffee filled the air and that told me Edi was up as well.

I got dressed, stumbled from my room, and cracked open the front door. "Lev, I'm gonna brush my teeth, grab coffee, and I'll be right out. I'm so sorry I slept in and didn't relieve you."

He replied in an almost monotone. "Fine."

Was he that tired, or was something wrong? No, he was mad. I left him on watch all night.

Hurriedly, I washed my face, brushed my teeth, then after kissing Katie, I grabbed a half cup of coffee and went to the porch.

"I'm sorry. I feel really bad."

Lev didn't even look at me. He was still sitting in the same spot I left him. "It's fine. I shut the alarm and light off," he said tonelessly, staring out.

"What? Why?'

"You looked tired and I wanted to be on watch all night."

"Well get some sleep now."

"I won't be sleeping. Not yet."

"Why?"

"Nila," he snapped, "pay attention to your surroundings." He pointed outward toward the fence.

I looked. I understood why Lev was there and knew then what he was staring out at. Parked outside our gate was a station wagon.

SEVEN

POST IT

July 31

I expected Lev to tell me that the station wagon had pulled up somewhere between brushing my teeth and coffee. That wasn't the case.

"Probably just when the sky got light," Lev said.

"Excuse me?"

"It wasn't completely light. I saw the headlights. They stopped."

"So they have been out there for, like, two hours?" I asked.

"Yeah."

It baffled me, both that they had been there so long and also that Lev was watching them.

"Is there a reason they're still there?"

Lev nodded. "They haven't gotten out yet."

"Is that the same station wagon from the Green?"

"I believe so, yes,"

I sat down next to him with my coffee. "What are we waiting for?"

"One of them to get out. I have a case of Nila right now."

"A case of Nila?"

"Yeah, I'm sitting here thinking whoever drove here just turned," Lev said. "Or if I approach they are gonna get out and shoot."

"Wow, that *is* my way of thinking."

"I hate that I even have that feeling," Lev said and looked at me. "But I have you, Katie, and Edi to worry about. You know?"

I nodded. "How about I go get the rifles?"

"Yeah. We'll both go in and get one, only you go out the back, take a sniper's position on the top of the old trailer. Don't let them see you. I'll head up to the gate. If they are trouble, you can take them out. If they are infected, I will."

"Sounds like a plan." I took another swig of my coffee and led the way back into the cabin. I proceeded to latch all the storm shutters.

"What's going on now?" Edi asked. "Another Lyssa?"

"No. Just stay inside," I said. I retrieved the rifles, Lev went to the front porch and I went out back.

I wondered how many people were in that wagon. Only one? Maybe more. When I climbed up on top of the trailer, I saw they had supplies and gas cans on the roof. I positioned myself belly down and used the scope of the rifle to get a good look.

Two people were in the front seat.

The second Lev walked near the gate. The driver's door opened and a man stepped out. The scope gave me a good close up. He had to be around fifty, maybe a few years older. His hair was cut short, gray, and his face had a scruffy beard.

He had a gun in a holster at his side. The second he stepped out, he lifted his hands.

I couldn't hear what they were saying, but whatever it was, the man put his hands down and Lev lowered his rifle. Then Lev turned, waved to me.

Obviously Lev had concluded the man was safe because he opened the gate.

I climbed down from the trailer, took the back way into the house, told Edi she could open the shutters but informed her to stay put as there were people at the gate and Lev just opened it.

While I trusted Lev's judgment, a part of me was upset that he opened the gate after such a short exchange of words.

As I stepped outside, the station wagon drew closer and Lev was walking behind it.

I waited on the porch for the wagon to stop. I could see two men in the front seat and heads of people in the back. They looked small.

The man stepped out.

"Thank you," he said. "We've been traveling a while. The big guy said to talk to you? I'm guessing the news isn't good?"

Admittedly, I was confused. What wasn't good? Then I saw Lev's face. He had a closed mouth smile as he came and stood by me.

The back door of the wagon opened and a boy jumped out.

My eyes widened. "Billy?"

Lev leaned down and whispered, "Aren't you glad we buried his father now?'

The small boy was not who I expected to see. How did he end up with this station wagon full of people?

"Billy here spotted the big guy when we were in Lancaster," the man said. "Ever try to find a place on the memory of a ten year old?" He smiled. "We were pretty close to here when we found Billy. I should have asked him then."

"Asked him what?" I questioned.

"About this place. We found Big Bear, but we didn't find this place. Mainly because it's not north."

"I'm sorry," I said, "I am really confused right now. Were you looking for *us*?"

"I was before I found Billy," he said. "Actually, I was looking for my son. He left a note on a survivor board. He was wrong, this place is south of Big Bear, not north."

"Your son?" I thought his son was Bill. I was floored to find out it wasn't.

"Yes. I'm Brian Cade," he said. "I'm looking for my son Brian Cade."

Once he said the name Cade I saw the resemblance between father and son. It was actually remarkable. Ben was a little taller than Cade, but was without a doubt an older, seasoned version.

I suppose it was because I was closest to Cade that Lev had left it up to me to break the news to Ben.

I explained to Ben that both of his children had passed. Julie by infection, and Cade was attacked. I told him that Cade had saved lives and was not only an asset, but a friend. I promised to share the pictures I took as well as stories.

He was saddened, of course, brokenhearted by the news. Though optimistic, he conveyed that he stayed realistic and somehow felt they were no longer with us.

At first I was baffled by how it was even possible. What were the odds that Cade's father would show up at our camp? Then after thinking about it and hearing his story, it made sense.

Ben and his wife were stranded in Erie when the city erupted into chaos. They couldn't get through the city barricades or hit the streets with all the infected. So they did what was the next best option, they attempted to get to safety via the lake.

Ben's friend and neighbor Gary had a boat, a bigger one. They loaded supplies and Ben and his wife, along with Gary and his wife, headed to the boat no more than ten blocks away.

The neighbor's son Corbin was already on board with his son waiting.

Mayhem was everywhere, yet they were confident. They unloaded the supplies and just as they prepared to move farther into the lake they were attacked by infected.

Cade's mother was bitten, and so was Gary. Neither was hurt badly, but the infection took over and while on board they turned.

"A lot of people had the same idea," Ben told me. "There were so many boats out there on the lake, it was insane. We all helped each other. Some went to Canada. A lot went to Canada. They say it's infection free."

"You came back for your son?"

Ben nodded. "I talked to Gary's family. Sue Ellen, Corbin, and Sawyer were up for whatever I wanted to do. I heard about the Greens through radio chatter. We waited months before coming ashore. Erie was quiet. Still some straggling infected, nothing dangerous that we couldn't outrun. I found a survivor wall, that's what I called it. People wrote messages. 'I'm alive. I'm here', things like that. I saw the name Cade, big and red. Under it was simply that he was at a cabin north of Big Bear."

"Cade went to find you but couldn't get into the city. He never mentioned he left word on a wall."

"Lots of people left word on that wall," Ben said.

"So there are people alive?"

"Billy was the only one we saw. We looked for this place, and couldn't find it. Found Billy on I79 looking for food. At first I thought he was infected. He said his father was bitten and ran off. We took him with us. Went to West Virginia first—there was no Green Area there—then Lancaster. We pulled inside and saw the infected. We were getting ready to hightail it when Billy recognized Lev."

"He went back to look for you," I said.

"We found you." Ben smiled. "Actually Billy was the one who said you weren't north of Big Bear, that you were south."

"Cade probably wrote it so fast," I said. "He was a good guy. I am so sorry for your loss."

"Did he suffer?" Ben asked.

At that second Lev approached and my eyes shifted to Lev before looking back at Ben.

"I'll take that as a yes," Ben said sadly.

"It wasn't for long," Lev said. "He was trying to help when it happened. It broke our hearts."

"Cade was such an asset to the group," I added. "He worked so hard helping people, treating them medically."

"Yeah, he should have been a doctor. I told him that, follow in my footsteps, but he didn't want to deal with the schooling," Ben said.

"We're glad to have you here," I told him.

"We won't be in your hair long. I just wanted to find my son."

"Then what?" Lev asked.

"People wrote down a lot of places they were headed. I made notes. I'm going to try for Canada," Ben said. "Radio chatter has it infection free, or at least they're beating it. Last place to get it knows how to fight it."

"If you are wrong," Lev said, "you'll be up there with limited supplies, with winter coming."

"It's a search for life, my friend," Ben said. "It's a goal. It's better than just sitting around."

"Is it?" Lev asked, then walked off.

I explained to Ben that Lev was pretty adamant that staying at the cabin was the right choice. Why would we gamble and leave where we were safe and self-sufficient.

"Is that what you want to do?" Ben asked.

"I want to do what's best for my daughter, what's safest for her. I can't bear to lose another child. If staying here for the time being is what is best, then that's what I'll do. Sure, I'm curious as to what's out there. Is my curiosity worth the risk with my daughter?"

"There's safety in numbers," Ben said. "I want to find a group of people."

"Correct me if I'm wrong, Ben, but five of you just stepped onto our land. Doesn't that now make *us* a group?"

It was funny, and it didn't hit me until after I said it. My father's cabin was a homestead. We had plenty of land, water, and safety. If we truly needed a community, a group, perhaps the answer wasn't going *out* to find a community, but rather being a community for people to find.

EIGHT

PLOTTED

Like a good soldier, Lev walked around the camp checking the fence, shining a flashlight out into the woods, and keeping an eye on everything.

After Lev's father, Lisa, and Hannah, died, we had moved the small trailer from the property and burned it. Lev got another from Big Bear, a small one they used to rent out to campers. Not only did he use that to keep watch, but that was his place.

Edi insisted on spending her nights in the old pop up, despite the fact she spent a lot of time during the day in the back air-conditioned room.

With both trailers on the property already, Lev suggested since Ben and his crew were only short term, instead of them setting up tents, that they take the small trailer. After all, it did sleep six. They agreed, and Lev moved into the cabin, taking the loft bedroom where Cade used to sleep.

Ben wasn't a much of a sleeper. He sat outside the trailer with Corbin while Sue Ellen and the boys slept inside.

I didn't know what to make of Corbin. He seemed nice enough. Judging by the age of his son, Corbin was probably a teenage father. He seemed like a good dad. He didn't speak much, and when he did, he didn't sound smart. I knew it was mean to think that, but he didn't have anything substantial or pertinent to add.

Maybe he liked to talk.

He and Ben went fishing and brought back enough for all. He told us over supper that before everything went bad, he was a maintenance man at department store in the mall. The 'light bulb' guy, he said. "Fastest changer this side of Cleveland."

I caught myself nodding and said, "Hmm," and before I said anything sarcastic, I humbled myself by remembering, before the virus, my job and claim to fame was 'fastest drive through cashier' at the local Arby's.

Who was I to judge?

"Nila, be nice," Lev said when I made a comment about Corbin that night as I walked with him.

"I am nice."

"No you're not. He is a good man. I can tell."

"I just have a different feeling."

"Such as?" Lev asked.

"I don't know. He asks weird questions. Like if we had a cat. Why would that matter? He's just strange."

"All this coming from a woman who takes survivor advice from Brad Pitt?"

"I'm not living that down, am I?"

"I will use it until it gets old and then some. You're being unnecessarily judgmental. I have never known you to be so shallow."

"Come on now, think about that," I said.

"Okay, you have been shallow before. They're good people. Ben is Cade's father. They went fishing, got food for all of us. Ben offered to take a watch shift tonight."

"You obviously aren't letting him." I said.

"I will after he knows the grounds. Then I can have a night to relax and beat you in chess. Come sit with me, I want to talk to you about something."

I followed Lev to the front of the house and joined him on the porch. We were invited to join Ben and Corbin when we walked by them. Lev was polite in declining.

"What's up?" I asked, sitting down.

"We have nine of us. Some are quite content staying right here. The rest are scattered in what they want, need, and should do."

"Lev, I understand your point about staying here and I'll stay."

"Yes, I know this. Staying is the safe option, this is the option we know is the best one. Mainly because we don't know what is out there. We don't have radio contact anymore, and all we have are tidbits of information of what may or may not be. Green areas, infection free places, things like that."

"What are you getting at?" I asked.

"Even though I don't want to leave, I would like to know other options. There is strength in numbers. Ben and Corbin are assets. A part of me does not want to lose contact with them."

"Wow, that's quite a thing for you to say. I always believed you had no doubts about keeping this camp safe and secure."

"Safe and secure, but I can't make you well. I can't help if there is an injury. I can't figure out what is wrong when someone falls ill."

"And Corbin can? He can fix light bulbs and stuff, not people."

Lev turned his head sideways and looked at me. "Did you miss the conversation with Ben? No, you didn't. You heard it, I heard it. Ben was talking about how Cade should have followed his footsteps."

"By going to school?"

"No, by being a doctor."

"I didn't get that from him."

Lev smiled. "I did and I asked. Ben is a doctor, and that is an asset we need."

"What kind of doctor?"

"Does it matter?"

"Yeah, I mean, if he's a plastic surgeon…"

"He still knows medicine. That's an asset to a group with children and elderly."

"You're confusing me, Lev. What are you getting at?"

"Ben wants to leave. I want to stay. Both of us are right and both of us are wrong. I stay, I am led to stay based on ignorance. Ben leaves, he is led to leave based on ignorance. None of us know for sure what is ahead in our choices. I was thinking of a compromise. Perhaps if we all know, then we can all make the intelligent choice."

"Compromise?"

"I wanted to see what your thoughts were about me suggesting to Ben that we do scouting parties."

His suggestion perked my interest. "You mean go out and look before we leap?'

"Yes. South, another Green area, or to Helena's camp. Why not cross the lake to Canada? Instead of an entire group, it is easier to move around with just a few."

"I like that idea. I like it a lot. Without any way to get information, this will be the best way to make us informed."

"Good. I'll talk to him tomorrow. And one other thing, just between you and me."

"What's that?"

"Bill was infected. We saw infected. We don't know if it was a reset, a new wave, or a mutation. We don't have Bobby to give us information. We aren't scientists, we can only learn from what we see. We learned a lot of how the body decayed, how fast, and when it ended by watching. We need to know what's out there to prepare and know what we are dealing with. You brought up that maybe they are alive longer if they eat. Billy's father was gone at least a week and was still in an infected state. How? What would you say if I suggested that should we find an infected, we...study it?"

"I'd say you're twisted." I paused. "But you're thinking ahead. So you're saying do a Pool Man Two?"

Lev looked at me and smiled. "Everyone loves a good sequel."

NINE

FROM LEV'S SIDE

Ben was a strong man, and not just intellectually. He was a pillar that wouldn't waiver. I could tell. He did all that he could to find his children and his mission now was to rest and go back out, search for life.

After Nila went to bed, I sat with Ben and Corbin. I explained my plan, how both of us were making our decision without full knowledge.

I don't know why I felt so strongly about Ben staying on. The fact that he was a doctor and we one, weighed on me. There were children, an elderly woman. What if someone got hurt or bitten? Did Nila and I possess enough knowledge to help heal? In the world, with it the way it was, I could hunt, provide food, water, but where would I take Nila, Katie, or Edi for help?

They were my responsibility, whether Nila accepted that or not.

Yet, if I were to be honest with myself, a part of me wanted it to be our tight little unit. Realistically, we needed others. They say it takes a village to raise a child; it takes a community to survive.

Needless to say, Ben declined.

Corbin had questions, but that didn't make an impact on Ben's decision. He seemed generally interested until he veered way off the subject and asked one of those obscure questions Nila was talking about. He'd asked earlier about cats, and in the middle of asking about search parties he asked if I ever considered playing major league baseball.

Ben wasn't the least bit interested in the prospect of search parties.

"I don't see the point," he said. "Two go out this week, two go out the next week. Seems like a lot of wasted time and resources. You wanna go, just go. Why scout it out? You seem like nice people. My only reason for coming here was my son. There's nothing that makes me want to stay now, or hang out any longer than I need to. Sorry."

I wanted to say, 'What about the fresh water, the lake, or the deer? The elements of survival."

I didn't.

I wasn't going to beg and I was somewhat insulted that we weren't good enough to stay with.

Although he would be an asset, we didn't need him. The longer I sat with him, the more bitter I became. We were offering him a safe place, sufficient food, and water, and still he declined.

To hell with him. He could leave. I'd figure out another way to find out what was out there.

I excused myself and continued my watch, staying clear of Ben and Corbin until Nila came out to relieve me. I didn't say anything to her about making the suggestion to Ben. I simply mentioned we would try harder with the radios in the morning and then I went to bed.

TEN

MINDSET

August 1

I don't know why there was such a feeling of safety and security the moment the sun started to rise. It was like the brighter sky brought less of a threat. I knew that wasn't true. While most of our attacks came during the daylight hours, the night was scarier.

I relieved Lev about two hours before daylight. We had a little rain, though not enough to make things muddy or interfere with the temperature. It was more of a nuisance. I was so happy to hear he really wanted to put forth an effort into making the radios work, even if we had to take them to the peak to try.

I spent most of my short shift walking or sitting on the roof of the RV. Once the sky started to lighten and I saw Ben and Corbin making coffee on the open fire, I said 'good morning' to them both and inquired about Sue Ellen and the boys.

Corbin asked me, "Have you ever watched the series finale of *Baywatch?*"

I told him I hadn't and let it be.

I sat on the porch with my folder and waited on Lev. He'd be out with his coffee soon and I'd go back to sleep for another hour or so. Sleep. Yes, I longed for that.

After writing down a detailed and impartial account of a moment, using a glue stick, I attached the picture that went with the historical narrative. Some entries didn't have pictures to go with them. Some pictures I didn't date.

On this particular morning, I was working on May fifth, nearly four months earlier. Most of the time, when I wrote the date on the back of the picture, I had to rely on memory. More than likely, I was off. May fifth, however, was a date forever logged in my mind.

I took a picture in my living room on that day, then one of the accident on my street. These I had already documented.

I looked at another photo I took on that day. Actually, Addy took it. It was of Cade wearing his backwards baseball cap, looking through his red bag. It wasn't a particularly good picture, slightly blurry, but a visual documentation nonetheless. It was not only the day we first met him, it was the day he and I went out looking for supplies.

I hadn't even realized Addy had taken a picture until I printed them.

Using that picture, I recounted the story on paper. How that was the day he had to take care of his sister Julie, who had turned in his car in our driveway, how he and I headed to Evans City but it was blocked off so we ended up at a veterinarian hospital to get much needed medical supplies. The trip was followed by a stop at Big Bear, where we got the radios.

It was a vital, long day. Besides being day one at the cabin, it was day one of the official infection.

I had the picture on the folder with a paper clip as I wrote, I would glue it when I was done.

It wasn't bright enough out to be a big one, but when a shadow fell across my book, I looked up, thinking Lev had come from behind the house. It was Ben.

"Morning," I said.

"Morning. Mind If I join you?" he asked, holding a cup of coffee."

"Please." I scooted over.

"I should have brought you coffee, I'm sorry. Can I get you some?"

"No. As soon as Lev is up, I'm going back to bed."

"What are you working on?"

I showed him the folder. "History. I want to write down as much as I can. That way there is a record. For me, for us, for the future. Who knows?"

"That's a good idea."

"Yeah, well, Cade joked about it. He and Lev used to make fun of me for taking pictures. I kept saying no one did this during the Spanish Flu epidemic."

"Is my son in any of these?" Ben asked.

I held the folder out to him. "He's is in a lot of these. This folder is the first month here."

Ben took the folder and opened it. "You started this when you first found out?"

"My brother Bobby was with the CDC, and I had a heads up on the virus. I had no clue what it was like in the beginning."

Ben flipped through and discovered that first picture of Cade. He lifted it and stared at it. "He truly was involved here."

"Yeah, he was. He was a part of our family and this whole place. He used to get so upset with my father because my father would make him chop wood and make spikes."

He chuckled. "Sounds like my son." He handed back the folder.

"Cade threw himself into the Big Bear wave of the virus. He helped out a lot there...he was bitten, you know."

"I figured that's how he died."

"No." I opened the folder, pulled out another picture, and handed it to him.

"A selfie?"

"That was taken in the car when he and I were trapped. He was stoned and convinced he was going to die because he had gotten bit on the ankle, but he never got sick. Either he was immune, or didn't get the virus because it needs a living host to be contagious. That was our theory,"

"He was bitten by a dead one?"

I nodded. "Months later he was attacked and there was no surviving the injuries. My heart broke. I feel him around here. Everywhere."

"What would he do?" Ben asked.

"About?"

"Staying? Going?"

"He'd eventually want to go, but he was pretty content here," I said. "He wasn't ready to leave. Why do you ask?"

"I just was…" Ben paused and looked behind us when the screen door opened and Lev stepped out.

"My relief has come," I said brightly.

"Don't know how much rest you'll get," Lev said as he stepped off the porch. "Katie is in full force."

"Already?" I asked.

"What can I say? She can make rounds and hang with me, I don't see any reason why there'd be trouble. I wanted to try the radio today and…" he peered up and moved clockwise. "The sky looks…"

I waited. "Lev? The sky looks what?"

"Shit."

"What?"

Ben stood up as well. "What do you see?"

Lev pointed out. "The hill up there. Big Bear."

"There's smoke," Ben said.

"Exactly," Lev said. "And there shouldn't be." He looked at me. "Someone is there."

ELEVEN

FROM LEV'S SIDE

It surprised me that Nila was so insistent that I did not go up to Big Bear, and that doing so was putting myself in a bad position. We all knew it wasn't the infected creating the smoke, and that had more dangerous possibilities.

I had no intention of going up and driving through the front gate. The smoke being emitted was intermittent and not heavy, so whoever it was didn't have a strong fire skill set.

Ben commented that it was probably one person who found the campsite and wasn't much of a camper. The early morning rain was probably making it impossible for them to get a good fire going.

My plan was to take the truck over to the Big Bear main entrance, pull it off to the side of the road a quarter mile beyond the driveway, and walk up through the woods to the camp. I knew my way around, I could go unnoticed and also slip into the camp without being seen. That way I would be able to see who was there, and how many had made themselves at home on my father's property.

I was armed and ready to go when for some reason not only Ben, but Nila, suggested I not go alone and for me to take Corbin.

"Are you good with guns?" I asked him.

"Not especially."

"Bow, arrow, knife?"

"Not really a weapons kind of guy."

I nodded. "I see."

"Is it important?"

I tilted my head left to right, not wanting to come off as sarcastic. "Could be."

"I'll give it a try."

"Why are you with me?"

"Safety in numbers," Corbin said.

I got in the truck and drove down the driveway to the main road. The whole time, I watched the smoke that emerged only every so often. Once we got to the main road, I couldn't see it anymore.

The ride was only a couple of minutes and conversation was nil until we pulled over and got out.

"Where are you from?" Corbin asked.

"I lived a good bit of the year in New York."

"City?"

"Yeah."

"Where are you from originally?" Corbin asked.

"Edgewood. It's a suburb of Pittsburgh,"

"Not that. I'm trying to place the accent."

"I don't have an accent."

He waved his finger. "Yeah, you do."

"You sound like Nila." I exhaled. "I was born in Serbia."

"Ah, okay, makes sense. I knew I heard a Russian accent."

I stopped walking. "I'm not Russian." I dropped my voice to a mumble. "Now for sure you sound like Nila."

He pointed. "Smoke's back."

I looked to the sky. "Yeah."

"You ever been in the Boy Scouts?"

I gave him an odd look, it was one of those questions Nila had been complaining about. "No."

"I have. Then again, don't you have to be an American citizen to be a Scout? Or is that you can't be gay?"

We weren't far from the camp. I followed the smoke and kept walking. "I believe you can be either and be a Scout. Besides, I am a citizen. My father is American."

"Funny thing about the Scouts…"

"Do you mind if we don't talk?"

"Oh, sure, yeah." He mocked zipping his mouth.

"Quiet is best in case there are a lot of people there."

His mouth tightly closed, he nodded.

We approached the camp from the west, coming behind the restrooms and showers near the community center.

Seeing it brought back memories of the day my father was bitten and Lisa was attacked. A good bit of the community center was still secure, which told me bodies were still inside. They had turned violent, and more than likely were now what we called corkers. It was quiet and I was trying to determine where the smoke was coming from.

There was a smell about the camp; rotten and putrid. When we came around the front of the community center, Corbin pointed to the body of an infected. Some of his limbs were black with necrosis. I could see those dark spider veins crawling across his cheek. He hadn't begun to fully decompose, so that told me he had been killed before the final stage, during the maddened stage while he was still alive. Fresh blood encircled his head.

"Looks like the new residents here are cleaning up," Corbin remarked.

I pulled out my weapon. I didn't see a group of people, in fact, I saw only a horse. Stepping closer quietly, I saw a thin stream of smoke, and when I veered to my right I saw a man by the fire.

I couldn't tell his age, or if he was injured or infected.

Lifting my rifle, I cleared my throat.

He sprang up and spun around. "Jesus!" he gasped and grabbed his chest. "Lev? Lev Boswick. Son of a bitch." He came my way.

Scott Gilner. I had known him since school when he and his family used to spend weekends in the summer up at Big Bear. Admittedly, I was in shock to see someone I hadn't been in contact with for ages. He looked the same. A little older, of course. We all were. Last I heard he was married and living somewhere in Kentucky.

Scott extended his hand with firm gratitude and stepped in to me for an embrace.

"You big son of a bitch," Scott said.

"Scott …what…what brings you here?"

"This is crazy. I…was looking for my parents."

Finally, I relaxed. His parents still occasionally came to the camp.

"I thought they may have come here," Scott said. "They weren't at the house."

I shook my head. "No, I'm sorry. They didn't come here at the onset. I haven't seen them."

Scott dropped his head. "Their house was torn apart. Lots of blood, I was hoping…I thought if I checked here, I might find them. This place was far enough away from the cities."

"It is. It was a good retreat spot," I said.

"Where is everyone?"

"They left. A lot got sick. The infection came with the people. We were never really safe."

"Shame." He looked around. "This could be a great place to wait it all out."

"I agree. Are you alone?" I asked.

"Yeah. I was at a Green area in Kentucky. It was overrun about six weeks ago."

"Six weeks?" I asked. "That's not long."

"It held up, but the infection came back. I lost my wife and two sons."

"I'm sorry, Scott," I said. "Truly sorry."

"Thank you." He extended a hand and stroked the calm horse. "At least I have Seltzer."

"Beautiful animal."

His eyes shifted to Corbin, who extended his hand and introduced himself, but gave no other details.

"Your father?" Scott asked.

"Passed away."

"I didn't know anyone was here. It didn't look like it," Scott said. "Were you out hunting?"

"Yeah," Corbin said. "We move around a lot." It was strange to hear Corbin outright lie like that. "So were you in the Boy Scouts with Lev?" Corbin asked.

Scott gave a weird look to Corbin and replied, "Um, I don't think Lev was in the Scouts with me."

"I wasn't," I said. "Actually, Corbin is new to our camp."

"Our?" Scott asked.

"Nila."

"Holy shit. Is she at her old man's property? I didn't even think to check there. Then again, why would I? That place didn't strike me as a long term place."

"We're doing well," I said. "We have a group. In fact, Nila will be happy to see you if you want to come down."

"I would appreciate that. I put my stuff in the office to make camp," he said, hooking a thumb in that direction. "I'll grab it. Can I bring Seltzer?"

"Absolutely, and I'll help you." I started to follow him and noticed Corbin was still by the fire. He stomped it out and was staring down. "You coming?"

"Yeah, yeah." He paused a moment, then said, "I was in the Boy Scouts. The whole thing. Cub Scouts, Boy Scouts. You should have been a Scout."

Stopping cold, I grunted. "I wasn't a Scout, so what, why does it matter?"

Corbin shrugged. "Cause you wouldn't have been so quick to tell him about the camp."

"I know him."

"Okay, but if you were in the Scouts—"

"Corbin!" I snapped.

He remained calm. "Lots of green in the fire makes white smoke, two spurts of smoke every thirty seconds. That damp rug." He pointed. "Two puffs of smoke, means location and safe. Had you been in the Scouts you may have noticed your friend was sending smoke signals. Just sayin'." He walked by me toward the office.

I looked down at the extinguished fire. Corbin was right, there was lots of green. Grass, branches with leaves, and beside it was a thin rug. I reached down for it and sure enough it was wet. I was amazed, Corbin's random questions actually held meaning. I didn't know the technical aspects, and I wasn't a Scout. Corbin couldn't be right. There was no way Scott was sending smoke signals. Why would he? The bigger question being, if by chance he was, who was he sending them to?

TWELVE

SPACE

I didn't really know Sue Ellen. Two days on my property and my opinion of her was that of a weak woman resigned to staying in the shadows.

That wasn't the case. The sixty year old mother to Corbin and grandmother to Sawyer was tired and cranky, and wasn't a particular fan of Ben's. An opinion that wasn't a recent one, they had been neighbors. Because of that she decided just to stay in the trailer until Ben noticed Edi had started coughing. He attributed it to the humidity and heat and ordered her to rest in the back room with the AC.

"It's not very apocalyptic," Ben said, "so take advantage of it. She needs to rest. I know she comes across pretty spry, but Edi is on the downside half of life."

I wasn't sure what he meant by that. Was she dying? I asked him that, to which he replied, "She's in her eighties, what do you think?"

I instantly felt grew depressed. How could Edi be well one day and at death's door the next? It was after my conversation with Ben that Sue Ellen came into the cabin.

After a few minutes, she emerged from the back room and went to the kitchen.

"I have been informed that in the best interest of your child, I should prepare lunch," she said.

"Oh my God, I'm not that bad."

Sue Ellen smiled. She had a warm face with short salt and pepper hair, yet her face sagged, making her look worn. I attributed it to losing her husband, stress, and possibly weight loss.

She had come to check on Edi and see if she needed anything, not because she was a nurse or anything, but because, as she put it, "Ben's bedside manner sucks."

"Really?" I asked.

"Oh, sure."

"Cade was so nice," I said.

"Brian, you mean?" she asked. 'Oh, he took after his mom."

"What kind of doctor was he?"

"A plastic surgeon."

"Ha!" I proclaimed loudly with a victorious slap of my hand to the counter. "I knew it."

"Don't let the title fool you. He knows his stuff. Wasn't always a vanity plastic surgeon." She turned to search the cabinets. "He used to help people who had injuries. I don't know what turned him to breast jobs. Ah, here, this must be what she meant." Sue Ellen brought out two jars and put them on the counter. One was dehydrated vegetables, the other was Edi's dehydrated stock.

"I could do that," I said, nodding to the jars.

"According to Edi you tried once and the vegetables were hard and the stock salty."

I shrugged. "You'll have that. If people are hungry, they'll eat it."

"You're fortunate to be in that position. This place is life," Sue Ellen said. "But is it fair to just assume there's no other life out there? I think Lev's proposal has merit and I think Ben will change his mind and go along with it."

"So Lev talked to him about the search parties? He didn't mention it, only that we had to try the radio again."

"They spoke early this morning," Sue Ellen said. "Corbin wants to do that. Ben wants to go to Canada. We would have been there already had we not been looking for Brian."

"What about you?" I asked.

"I want what's best for my grandson and son. I've got to see a little of what's out there and there's nothing but death. Maybe in a few years things will grow again, not now. Not with those things still there. We spent months on that boat. We had all we needed but it wasn't a picnic."

"And Ben is convinced about Canada?"

"For sure." Her head turned at the same time the sound caught my attention. "Was that a horse?" she asked.

Having also heard the neigh, I hurried to the front door. When I opened it, I saw Lev driving through the gate, Ben stood off to the side holding it, and already on the property was a man on horseback. After my initial thought of 'where the hell are we gonna keep a horse?' I recognized the rider.

Seeing someone from the past not only was a shock, but a glimmer of hope. There were indeed more people out there.

Although I had known Scott since grade school, I wasn't inclined to run to him and wholeheartedly embrace him like a long lost love. It was good to see him and I did give him a quick hug.

I wasn't surprised that he went to Big Bear. It sat higher than my cabin and wasn't as enclosed. It made sense he never saw smoke from our camp, then again, neither did Ben, and they were looking for us.

The horse was beautiful, brown and silky. The kids were excited and raced out to see him. I kept them back because I wasn't sure how the horse would respond to the kids.

They reached out timidly to touch his mane. He was very calm and gentle and I held onto his reins, surrounded by the kids, while Lev took Scott and showed him where he could clean up and set up his tent. Our fenced in property was a decent size, but it surprised me that Lev wasn't even inviting Scott into the cabin.

"Can I ride him, Mommy?" Katie asked.

"Oh, I don't know. He's not mine so I can't say. But if you're allowed, let me take him out and judge."

Corbin asked. "You ride?"

I nodded. "I'm not great, it has been a while."

At that moment, Lev returned. "I have him set away from Edi's camper. Don't want her chickens to bother him."

Both Lev and I looked quickly at Corbin, who snickered.

Lev reached out and stroked the horse's nose. "His name is Seltzer."

"He's a thoroughbred," I said. "We don't have enough land here for him. What are we gonna do if Scott stays?"

"We can build a fenced in area in the back and he's gonna need turnout," Lev said. "Most of the day he needs to be out. He's pretty calm, so I don't see him running amok. We can take him out or Scott can. We just have to watch the roads. He already made the trip hundreds of miles on concrete. I'm surprised he's still walking well."

"We can take him up to Big Bear," I suggested. "The trails are still there from when your father had horses."

Lev nodded. "Could. Depends if Scott stays."

"Odd isn't it?" I asked. "That he ended up at Big Bear?"

"He was looking for his family."

"Yeah, but Scott? Maybe he changed, but he was a terrible camper. Hated it. Hell, he got kicked out of Boy Scouts."

Corbin snorted a laugh. . "Well he picked up something from it. Hey, do you cut hair?"

"No," I answered.

"Didn't think so. Maybe I'll have the doc have a go at it. He's good with shaping things." He clapped his hands together once. "Hey, kids, I found a pair of clippers. Who wants to help me cut my hair?"

Sawyer, Billy, and Katie all screamed excitedly that they did.

"Let's go." Corbin waved them to follow. "Hey, Lev, tell her about the Scouts."

Lev groaned as Corbin led the kids toward the RV.

"Lev, he is so strange."

"You think?"

"Out of the blue he wants a haircut and he's gonna let the kids cut his hair?"

"I can't imagine it would be any worse than it is. Walk with me," Lev said, taking the rein of the horse and leading the way.

I had to laugh at Lev's comment. It was funny coming from a man who cropped his hair so short it stuck up everywhere.

"What's going on?" I asked.

"Corbin wants to talk Ben into staying for a little bit. Maybe doing some scouting trips with me."

"That's good," I said. "Sue Ellen isn't a fan of leaving yet either. But this isn't what you want to talk to me about, is it?"

Lev shook his head. "Corbin thinks that Scott was sending smoke signals. It's the top of the highest point, it could be seen for miles."

I stopped walking. "That sounds absurd. What do you think?"

"I don't know what to think. I don't know about making smoke signals. Corbin seems to think he had the makings."

"Corbin?"

"He was in the Boy Scouts."

"Okay. But why?" I asked. "Why send signals?"

"Maybe he's with a larger group, doesn't have a radio, and this was his sign to them that he found a place."

"If he was with a larger group, why come with us? Why not say something?"

Lev stopped walking. "Because maybe Big Bear isn't what they want."

It took me a second and then I laughed at the notion. "You mean this place?"

"Yes. We have water, food, safety. We can sustain life here indefinitely."

"Lev, really, who knows about this place and what we have?" Before Lev could answer, it came to me. "Oh, shit. All the radio contacts I made."

"Yep."

"I lost contact with them."

"We can't rule it out. The last they knew, you were leaving." Lev started walking the horse again. "We just remain diligent."

Scott? No way. No how. He was just a lost soul looking for his family and trying to survive.

I heard Lev's words, but the more I thought about it, the more I believed we were overthinking and possibly paranoid. Being neurotic about it was easy. Movies and books showed us there was no peace in a dead world. Where there was life, there was always someone who would want to take it. Our camp was secluded, isolated, and small. However, if by some chance Corbin was right and Scott was sending signals, our little haven wasn't as secluded and safe as we hoped it would be.

THIRTEEN

TANGLED

August 8

It lunged with speed and energy like I had never seen an infected move. His head cocked and he sniffed loudly. He sensed we were watching him and was trying to catch our scent. The man, who was about thirty, was still very much alive, infected, and had entered the rabid stage. His skin was pasty white, dark veins looked like a roadmap on his face. He was obviously infected through a bite on his arm. That wound hadn't healed and. The entire arm was black and oozing.

We watched him through a small opening where he moved freely about the inside of a ten by twelve shed. It was a pre-fabricated unit Lev picked up from the home store on the highway south of us. Lev and Corbin put it together, erecting it outside the fence of my father's property. Lev bitched because he had just gone down to that same home store the day before to get a shed that he reconstructed to work as a small stall for Seltzer.

"I swear to God, Nila,' Lev said. "All I do is build things on this property."

That was true, though Corbin helped with both sheds, and surprisingly they were his idea. It was also his idea to move the station wagon off the property in the middle of the night.

"Just in case," Corbin said.

I didn't understand but I didn't bother to question further. Corbin had a method to his madness I was still trying to figure out.

How we came to acquire the infected was part of that madness.

It all started because Scott hadn't done much. He slipped into some sort of quiet depression, avoiding most of us and keeping to himself. He attributed his behavior to adjustment. It wasn't that long before, weeks maybe, that he had lost his entire family, and it was the first time he had stopped moving since. It was just hitting him and he was absorbing it all.

Ben tried talking to him, and I blamed Ben's crass manner for the reason Scott was doing so badly. So much so he seemed to forget about the horse he brought with him.

Right after we got the shed for Seltzer, Lev, Corbin, and me worked out turnout times, each of us taking turns walking the horse or riding him outside and close to the perimeter of camp.

With Ben and the others deciding to stay and plan scouting parties, we were quickly establishing a rapport and routine. Edi was getting better, Sue Ellen was teaching the kids, and I monitored the radio.

On Scott's third day at our camp, Corbin took Seltzer out for an afternoon ride. He was gone for hours, long enough for Lev to get concerned and start prepping the truck.

Just before sundown Corbin trotted to the gate with a bouncing body slung over Seltzer's back. The body was partially on Corbin's lap. I thought for sure he found a body and wanted to add it to our little graveyard until he hollered out to Lev, "Hey, I got something for you!" and the body started to writhe. It was then I noticed the male body was bound at the hands and feet.

My second thought was Corbin had kidnapped someone. Then that same body shook violently, growling each time until he convulsed hard enough to fall off the horse, land hard on the ground, and was rendered unconscious.

"Oh good." Corbin dismounted. "I don't have to knock him out again."

"Again?" Lev asked,

"Yeah. I had to hit him like three times since I found him to knock him out. My hand hurts. It might be broke. Probably not, but it hurts." He opened and closed his fist a few times. "I think we ought to figure out what to do with him pretty quick. He gets more agitated every time he wakes. He's feisty."

Lev was fuming. For a moment he stared. He looked away once, to glance over his shoulder and ask Ben to make sure everyone was safe inside the cabin. He even told me to go inside, but I wasn't about to miss the exchange between him and Corbin.

"You brought an infected onto the property?" Lev asked. "Why?"

"Nila told me you wanted to study them, see if the infection mutated. I thought it was a great idea, then you never said anything more about it. I thought you forgot or were just scared to get one."

"You did tell me that," I said. "Not about you being scared to get one, about wanting to watch one."

"What?" Lev asked in confusion.

"Pool Man Two, the sequel?" I said, trying to refresh his memory.

"Hey!" Corbin snapped his fingers. "I've got an idea." He then yelled, "Ben! What do you have to keep this thing unconscious for—"

"Shh!" Lev hushed him.

"Why am I being quiet?" Corbin asked. "He's out." He nudged the infected with his foot.

"You suggested we learn the enemy," I said. "We have our chance. Kill it or learn from it?"

Lev shook his head. "I don't know."

"How did you find him?" I asked. "Do you think there's more?"

"I didn't see any," Corbin replied. "I was taking Seltzer down the driveway, thought I'd take him along the road up to Big Bear. Before I got there I saw a car."

"A car?" Lev said, his interest piqued. "Where?"

"By Big Bear. It looked like it had run off the road," Corbin said. "At first I thought it was because of Scott's smoke signals, then I knew something was wrong. There was a woman in the front seat. She was dead. I could tell by the black lines on her face she was infected, but her entire chest was torn apart."

I cringed.

"Then I saw our friend here," Corbin nodded downward. "He was having lunch on his kid. I thought of what you said about learning them and hit him with my gun. The rest is history. Here we are."

At that moment Ben came over with a syringe. "This will keep him out for a couple of hours. Should I give it to him?"

"No," Lev said. "Don't waste it."

Then I saw the face of the infected man. "Wait. Corbin, you said he was with a woman and a child near Big Bear?"

"Yes."

"Lev," I said, "that's Lester Williams. He left Big Bear with his family that day your dad got bit. You got into a fight with him about taking supplies."

"Shit," Lev whispered.

"Yeah, like Bill. He left and came back, which means he has to know. The infected have to know what they're doing. Hell, he may even have driven the car. That's a scary thought."

"That's impossible," Lev said. "He was probably like Bobby, got sick, and died close to his destination."

"What if that's not the case? What if the infection stage isn't just lasting longer, they aren't only rage driven, they're enraged and intelligent?"

Corbin whistled. "Wow, staying alive just got harder."

Infected Lester growled.

"What am I doing?" Ben asked.

After a beat, Lev answered. "Knock him out."

Ben administered the morphine, then reluctantly at our request examined Lester.

"This bite is about four days old," Ben determined. "So he turned into the rabid stage probably yesterday, day before at most."

"That's still longer than the initial outbreak," I said.

"Not by much," Ben countered.

"Which means he probably was sick, turned, and crashed his car right before getting to Big Bear," Lev said. "Four days doesn't prove that he went there on memory."

"I highly doubt that," Ben said. "The fever alone makes them unable to comprehend. Yes, he's lived longer than he should have, but..." Ben shook his head, "I don't see him lasting in this state much longer. The infection and necrosis is in his veins. He'll probably make the turn into the dead phase tonight."

That was days earlier.

Now we stood, on the fifth day of being in possession of Lester, building him a home and feeding him small animals while studying him and learning.

Lester was still in the rabid infected stage. Still going strong and showing no signs of moving into the death phase anytime soon.

FOURTEEN

FROM LEV'S SIDE

I distinctly remember being told that when Nila's father Earl was stockpiling for the retreat to the cabin, that he had purchased so much ammunition he was flagged by Homeland Security. Yet as I stood in the shed with Nila, I was amazed at how little ammo we did have.

"Does this look right?" I asked her, shaking a half empty box of shells.

"I don't know."

"You said there was a lot."

"When was the last time we counted?" she asked.

"Don't know that we ever counted," I said. "I just know there was more than this when we left."

"When we returned, did we leave some on the truck, maybe lose some?"

"I doubt it," I said.

"You don't think someone is stealing it, do you?"

"Who?" I asked. "I find it hard to believe any of them would steal. They aren't going anywhere."

"Can we get more? You and Corbin are doing the first scouting party next week."

"We're gonna have to," I said. "Hopefully find a place that isn't picked clean."

"You know, for a dead world, things *are* awfully picked clean. Who did it, and where are they?"

"I don't know who, but more than likely they are like Lester."

"Maybe they're not. Maybe they're out there. We just need to find them."

I shut the bin that held the ammunition. "Maybe."

"Ah, you're coming around on this."

"There's no coming around. One day everyone wants to stay, the next Ben is talking about Canada again."

"He says there's a reason we need to get there and it's not just because there's supposed to be life there."

"Yes, well, Canada is cold. I can't see there being too much life there come winter."

"What if what he heard is right?" she asked. "Maybe the reason we can't find those people who picked over everything is because they went to Canada and it's infection free."

"How could that be?"

"I hear they have great healthcare."

I laughed and shook my head at her bad joke. Assuming it was a bad joke; there was a chance that Nila wasn't joking,

She sighed as if she were done with me and stepped back. "Was that all you needed? To ask me about ammo?"

"You act like I bother you."

Nila looked up and smiled. "Never."

"Thank you."

"I want to get back to the radio and I still need to deal with Edi."

"How is she feeling today?"

"Better. Enough to say she wants to go back to her trailer. I keep telling her she will smell Lester from there but she's stubborn."

"Maybe have Ben talk to her."

Nila laughed. "She found out he was a plastic surgeon and her attitude changed. She said when she needs a breast lift then she'll listen to Ben."

For some reason that made me wince. Nila headed back to the cabin and I stuck the extra rounds of ammunition in my pocket. Not that I needed it, but I wanted to have it handy when I walked outside the fence for my daily assessment of Lester.

Part of me wished I would have put him in the pool house up at Big Bear, but it really would have been too much going back and forth to check on him.

Corbin joined me. He seemed to get some sort of sick enjoyment out of the daily checks on our infected guest.

"Day six," Corbin said after snapping a picture with Nila's phone.

"Why is she having you take pictures?" I asked.

"She said she is comparing them and it makes a good record."

"Does he look different to you?" I asked.

"No. Not at all."

I peered in our observation window. Lester was always agitated, moving constantly. He smelled so badly that my eyes watered even if I looked through that window only briefly.

"Are you gonna try it today?" Corbin asked. "You should before he dies."

"Yes," I told him.

I knew what he was referring to. After Corbin brought him to the camp, the next day I went down to take care of his family. I found Lester's wallet, and in it were pictures. I wanted to try and see if he recognized anyone. I had put it off, maybe part of me was scared that there was a memory in that deranged body. A thinking infected was a scary thought.

I pulled out the wallet.

After flipping through, I took out the license and held it up to the small opening.

Nothing. Next was the picture of his son, I even called out, "Look, Lester, it's your kid."

He flung himself violently toward me.

Credit cards, a debit card, then finally, when I held up the picture of his wife, he stopped.

Lester grew quiet and calmly walked toward me.

"He knows her," I said. "He remembers her."

"Everyone remembers a good meal," Corbin replied.

"Did you really just say that?"

"I did. And I'm getting sick. I can take a lot, but this stinks too bad for me. I came armed."

He whipped out a can of Lysol and proceeded to spray it continuously into the opening.

Lester started to cough.

"You hear that?" Corbin said. "He's coughing. His reflexes are still good."

"He's still alive, six days later. Why is that?" I handed Lester the picture. Surprisingly, he put it right in his mouth and ate it.

Corbin pointed. "See? I told you. He remembers a good meal."

I gave up on Lester when I saw Ben walking the horse. He didn't ride, but he also didn't mind walking Seltzer when he was on watch.

We joined him on the inside of the fenced in area.

"I see you were visiting our friend," Ben said. "Not dead yet?"

"No, and that's what I wanted to speak to you about," I replied.

"He'll go any day now." Ben nodded. "I'm sure."

"Didn't you say that the other day?"

Ben winked. "If I say it every day, I'll eventually be right."

"Why do you think this is?" I asked. "I saw how sick people get. Why is Lester still alive?"

"You saw how sick people get after the bite, before they turn rabid," Ben said. "Very rarely do people die from the onset of symptoms. The virus mutated, plain and simple. A virus is not meant to die. When the host dies, so does the virus, so it's trying to stay alive longer. It adapted to survive. Sort of like you have a pot of water. You keep it on the highest flame it will boil down faster. Lower flame, it takes longer. The virus simply turned down to survive. Honestly, though, you're dancing on inhumane territory. I know you want to see how much longer this lasts. Assume a long time, and put the man out of his misery. We got the answers we were looking for. It mutated. For all we know the method of transmission could have changed."

"Airborne?"

"We don't know. That's why we need to get to Canada." Ben shifted his eyes to Corbin, then back to me. "There are answers there."

"You are very certain about this. You don't even have proof."

"It's a strong gut instinct and we have reason to follow that."

"Why is that?"

"Lev!" Sue Ellen called, and came running from the cabin.

My attention was drawn to her. "What is it?"

She caught her breath. "Nila made contact on the radio."

I ran into the cabin. Nila was sitting in the front room smiling as she held the radio. I mouthed the word, "Who?"

She released the button on the microphone. "Helena. The Kentucky camp."

It had been weeks since we heard from her.

"So things are good?" Nila asked her.

"Very good now. It was touch and go for a bit, Sweet Pea," Helena said. *"But we're back on our feet and got things running again. We're in a temporary camp now. We found a new place and are heading there."*

"Canada?'

"Not yet," she said. *"I want to get through on the radio first."*

They chatted for a little bit more. Nila seemed thrilled to hear from her. I would have been as well, had something not seemed…off.

For months I heard Nila talking with Helena, but this call was different. The sound of Helena's voice was crystal clear. No static, no interference. It was almost as if Helena was close. Very close. And since Helena knew our approximate location, if she was that close, why didn't she say anything?

FIFTEEN

PIECES

August 10

The sense of normalcy, if you could even call it that, was going to be short lived, or at least placed temporarily on hold. There were four of us making rounds, but Lev and Corbin planned on leaving in two days for the first scouting trip, aiming to go southwest. Ben really wanted them to go north, but according to him, they'd have to go deeper into Canada to find infection free zones. Places, he had heard, were working on a cure.

Once they left, that would leave only me and Ben to split the shifts. I was getting used to sleeping, and not only that, having Lev get some sleep.

There were nights I'd be on the verge of sleeping and I would hear him tromp about to his loft bedroom. Or if he knew I was still awake, he'd pop in my room to say goodnight.

The night before, he stopped in, lay horizontally across the bottom of my bed, head propped on his hand and we talked. We talked about a lot of things, where he was headed, what Lester was up to, how Katie was starting to read... then, mid-conversation, he fell asleep.

I left him there and covered him with a blanket. Not only did I not want to disturb him, I liked having him around and close. That was the reason I got up early. It was my day to turnout Seltzer and I wanted to get that done before Lev woke up. I just wanted to spend time with my friend. I felt we had become complacent, kind of rolling with the punches of life.

I waved to Corbin as I walked out to the back, lit the water heater, and noticed Scott wasn't there, but Seltzer was.

"Corbin," I called out, and he came around the back.

"Where's Scott?" I asked, untying Seltzer.

"He went fishing about two hours ago."

"Why didn't take Seltzer?"

"He said he didn't want to."

"That's odd." It was then a breeze swept in and with it came the smell of rotting flesh mixed with a sour, pungent smell. "Did Lester die?"

"Not that I know of, why?"

I sniffed. "You don't smell that?"

"It's probably Lester. But to be on the safe side, don't take Seltzer out. Wait for Lev to get up, we'll check the area, make sure there aren't any deaders."

I laughed as I mounted the horse. "I have a gun. I can handle the dead."

"Yeah as long as it's only a few."

"I'm on a horse, I can move fast. No worries. Besides, I want to find Scott. If there are any infected out there, he may not be ready for them. You know how he's been."

"Let me go with you."

"No. Don't be silly." I rode to the gate at a slow pace while Corbin walked beside me. "We haven't seen an infected since you brought Lester here over a week ago."

"We also haven't checked the area in four days."

89

"Open the gate," I said. "It's fine. I'll stay on the roads and trails where I can't get trapped."

Reluctantly, Corbin did, but I sensed he wasn't going to sit back and wait. I had a feeling that he'd wake either Ben or Lev. In either case it wouldn't be long until Corbin was coming after me with the truck.

I really wasn't worried. I could smell that there were only a few in the area, and I wasn't scared. I actually liked the feeling of not being scared.

I rode down the driveway, keeping a vigilant eye out for any infected. I didn't see any. Once I hit the main road, I turned as if going to Big Bear. A quarter mile down, hidden between our two driveways was Lake Trail Road, a dirt road that led to the lake. It was big hike for Scott. Even Lev took the truck because of the heat.

I attributed him walking to the fact that he hadn't been out of our camp or far from his little tent since he arrived. He needed to get out. Maybe Scott had come out of his shell.

Still, having spent most of my life up within those hills, I knew it was a good three mile hike from our driveway down to the main road and along to Lake Trail Road. Unless Scott went through the forest, that would have cut his trip in half.

Lake Trail was narrow, overgrown, winding, and the first half was uphill. I had just made the first bend when I stopped. I swore I heard a car. It was moving fast and I waited a moment and listened. I could still hear the engine sound, but it faded. It had to be Corbin. He'd wasted no time following me, but somehow he missed Lake Trail. I guessed it wouldn't be long before he came barreling down, trying to make it on the narrow road.

I kept Seltzer at a four beat walk, a slow, steady pace so he would make it up the large grade without tiring. Just as we did, I spotted a group of infected off the trail and in the woods. There had to be at least eight of them. I wasn't sure if they were in the infected stage or deaders. I wasn't taking any chances. I picked up the pace. They didn't pursue me, which was a good thing. I worried that Scott somehow was overrun, or was fishing and unaware they were so close.

I made it to the downside of the hill and knew I had lost them. I kept up a faster pace until I made it down to the lake.

When I got there I didn't see Scott at all. That didn't mean he wasn't there, he could have been at the far end, which would have made sense if he cut through the woods to get there.

I rode the edge of the lake wanting to call out, but knowing it was best not to. Even before the virus hit the lake was always peaceful and quiet. Being set in the hollows of the hills, sound traveled even more. It wasn't always possible to pinpoint the direction of the sound however, in a dead world sound didn't just travel, it was amplified. When the first shot rang out it startled me, and caused Seltzer to buck.

The single shot echoed through the hills. My first thought was the infected had reached our camp until a woman's scream carried out, followed by a barrage of gunfire.

Seltzer went nuts. He lifted up his hind legs, nearly throwing me off. I gained control of him, and with a snap of the reins headed full speed back to the road. My heart raced, fearful for my family. The gunfire still rang out. I quickly made it up the crest of the hill.

As soon as I made it over the top, I ran right into a horde of infected that blocked the road. They had come from the woods at the sound of the gunfire.

They weren't deaders, or Lyssa, they were infected, rabid, and were coming at me.

I couldn't go forward, I couldn't go back. Arms reached and grabbed, I kicked out, trying to push them away. I wanted to grab my gun, but it took everything I had to control Seltzer. I didn't want him to throw me. Seltzer lifted up, turning left then right. He was scared. He went from neighing to almost a roar. Finally, I snapped the reins and veered him to the right. He plowed through the group of infected and raced into the wooded area off the road.

I kept going, darting in and out of the trees, not paying much attention to where I was. The infected ran after us, crying and squealing. We moved faster than they did and eventually I lost them.

I stopped to not only catch my breath, but to get my bearings. My heart was beating out of control and I could feel it in my throat.

Not sure exactly where I was, I looked to the sky for some sort of direction.

I spent my life in those woods, yet tossed deep within them in a state of panic, I might as well have been on foreign land.

Seltzer walked sluggishly, the ordeal had frightened him. He was hard to control and after a good fifteen minutes of moving through the woods, we emerged back on to Lake Trail Road, nearly being run over by Lev's truck as it came down the hill.

Corbin was driving and he screeched to a stop. "Jesus," he said. "I was looking for you. I got scared. I couldn't get by the infected."

"Did you hear the shots?" I asked. "How could I not?"

"Is that why you came for me?"

"No, Ben sent me after you right away."

"We have to…" From the corner of my eye I saw the infected running down the hill. "We have to get back!" I guided Seltzer out in front of the truck and took off.

Corbin tried to say something to me. I didn't hear him.

Once I hit the main road, he stayed at the same pace as me. He could have passed me, but I suppose he didn't want me out of his sight.

Seltzer slowed as I came close to my driveway. "Little more, boy, just a little more. I know you're tired."

Turning up our driveway, Corbin was right on my heels. I moved over to let him pass me. If there was trouble with infected, we needed to get back right away. One of us had to get there.

By the time I made it to the open gates, Corbin was already in the camp and the truck was stopped fifteen feet from the cabin.

"No!" Corbin screamed, grabbing his head. It was a heart wrenching, panicked scream.

I jumped from Seltzer and pulled my revolver. At the side of the cabin was an infected woman. She was on her knees above a body. I couldn't see who it was, all I saw was blood.

Raising my weapon, I headed to the infected. She lifted her head and that was when I saw that beneath her was Edi. Poor Edi. Her frail body was torn to shreds.

Before the infected woman could lunge, I fired one shot, taking her out.

"Nila!" Corbin hollered. "Oh, God."

I tried to process what all had happened.

When I was at the lake, I heard the scream. Then I heard all that gunfire. If there was that much of an exchange, where were the bodies of the infected? Why was there only one in the camp?

Where was my daughter? Lev? The others? Billy, Sawyer, Ben, and Sue Ellen?

I ran to the cabin, and as I hit the front porch, I saw Sue Ellen's body. She lay face down, her body covered in blood.

The door of the cabin was open and when I stepped onto the porch, I stepped in blood.

"No, no, no!" I screamed inside and flew into the cabin.

"Oh God, oh God!" Corbin raced about the cabin, as if searching. "Sawyer!"

It was all happening too much too fast.

Edi was dead at the hands of an infected. Sue Ellen was dead. Corbin was crying out for his son. I didn't see my daughter and to my horror, Lev lay in the middle of the floor.

A trail of blood led from the porch to Lev. Obviously, whatever happened to him, happened outside and he'd crawled in.

"Lev!" I dropped to my knees by him. There was blood on his arm, his leg, and it was pouring from his stomach. "Lev!"

"Where are they?" Corbin asked frantically. "Where are the kids?"

I was trying not to panic, I believed with every ounce of my being that Lev would have protected the kids. "Lev?" I whimpered, moving my hand to his neck.

Before I could feel for a pulse, I saw his shoulders move. He was alive and wasn't bitten by any infected. It was obvious Lev had been shot multiple times.

"Where are they!" Corbin shouted. "They aren't here! Where are they? Nila, our kids!"

"I know." It was hard to even breathe. "Look outside," I suggested, trying to put my hands somewhere on Lev that would stop the bleeding, but I was at a loss.

"I can't... my mom, she's... I can't lose my son," Corbin said in a rush. "I can't lose my child."

I closed my eyes tight. "I can't either. Please look outside."

Our best answer to the whereabouts of the kids was with Lev. I had to get him to respond.

"Lev," I called him.

Right when Corbin opened the front door, we heard, "Daddy?"

Corbin ran back in the cabin. "Sawyer!"

"Dad!"

"Mommy!" Katie called out.

I looked around, Corbin looked around—neither of us saw the kids. And then it hit me. Lev wasn't just laying in the middle of the floor, the floorboard storage was directly under him.

"Oh my God!" I said. "The storage. Help me move Lev."

Corbin rushed over, grabbed Lev under the shoulders, and I took hold of his feet. We moved him over enough to expose the handle of the floorboard storage area hatch.

I hurriedly lifted it. There, squashed together, nearly on top of each other amongst the hidden supplies were the three children.

I heaved out a breath of relief when Katie reached out, realizing at that moment that my amazing, beautiful friend not only hid the children, but after taking several bullets, made his way into the cabin to ensure whoever attacked us, never found them.

SIXTEEN

HEAD DOWN

Through it all, there were moments I believed were a godsend.

Finding the children safe was one of them, another was when Ben emerged from the outhouse.

His face was covered with blood, his footing unsteady, and his eyes glazed. Yet he was the best and only chance we had at saving Lev.

My friend was dying. While his heart was beating and he was taking shallow breaths, he didn't respond. I didn't know if he ever would. There was so much left to say, to do, how was I to face everything ahead of me without him? That wasn't an option or a scenario I would easily accept.

It was obvious by Ben's appearance and reaction that he wasn't cowering and hiding in the bathroom. He stumbled out and fell to his knees, because the first thing he saw had to be Edi and the dead infected.

We only knew he had emerged because we heard him.

"Ben!" I gasped. "Thank God. That has to be Ben."

My hand stayed on Lev's stomach wound, while Katie's tiny hand pressed to his leg.

"Is he gonna die, Mommy?" she asked

"I hope not, baby."

Corbin returned with Ben. It was apparent Ben was still taking in what had occurred. He stumbled and knelt down on the floor.

"You all right?" I asked him.

He blinked several times trying to focus. "Yeah. Yeah. I will be. Give me a moment."

I wanted to ask him what happened, but he focused on Lev. He instructed the kids to go in the other room and Corbin to go get his bag.

"The big one," he said. "We're not gonna have time to move him and this is our OR." Ben turned to me. "I need hot water. A huge pot."

He took over the wound care and I stood quickly and headed to the kitchen. That was when I noticed every cabinet door was wide open and every one that had contained food was bare. I paused for a moment, but I couldn't deal with that right then. I grabbed the water pot from the stove and took it to the back porch to get the water from the heater. Thankfully, it was hot. I had lit the fire before I left.

After filling it, I carried the pot inside and set it next to Ben. Corbin was already back, the big bag so reminiscent of Cade's open on the floor.

"How is he?" I asked.

"I'll know in a bit." Ben forced a smile while preparing an IV. "Why don't you take the kids to my trailer while we work on him?"

"Mom's out...out front." Corbin choked on his words. "I didn't get to move her."

There was a cedar chest by the window where we kept blankets. I retrieved one and stepped outside. My foot hit the porch and I slid a little on the blood.

All that blood.

Blanket in hand, I stepped off the porch and heard the weakened neigh at the same time I saw Seltzer. If my heart wasn't breaking already, it was crushed when I saw that beautiful animal laying on his side. He lifted his head and tried to stand, only to fall again.

Sue Ellen's bullet riddled body was between the cabin and the trailer.

My God, why would they shoot her like that? She wasn't a threat. I dropped the blanket, clutched her under her arms, and pulled her a little away from the front so the kids wouldn't see.

She didn't even look peaceful. Her eyes were wide open and her face held fear. "I'm so sorry," I said, closed her eyes, and covered her with the blanket.

With the addition of Sue Ellen and Edi, our cemetery was growing.

My father's paradise, his escape, our sanctuary was crumbling.

Seltzer's call caught my attention again and I walked over to him. What had happened? Was he shot? Had he twisted his leg? When I got closer, I saw that he had probably just dropped when I jumped from him. His silky coat was wet with blood, his eyes were bloodshot, and I noticed the bite and tear marks all over his hind legs and side.

The infected had got him when they encircled us, biting and clawing him. No wonder he jumped and cried out so much.

Poor Seltzer. He kept looking at me as if crying out for help, begging me to do something.

How could I put him down? I didn't have it in me to lift my gun and I certainly didn't want to ask Corbin. He had just lost his mother.

So much death, and now Lev's life hung in the balance.

I wanted to believe Seltzer was fixable, but I could see tendons and bone, and his eyes had the look of infection.

Then I remembered the vials containing the euthanasia solution Cade and I got from the veterinary hospital. We never used them all. They were in the closet by the small back bedroom.

If, that was, they hadn't been taken as well. I returned to the cabin, entering through the back door. I would have to cover Edi as well once I got the kids into the other trailer. I felt as if I were disrespecting her, leaving her there.

I noticed her chickens were gone as well. Of course, they were. Those chickens were a good source of food.

Entering through the kitchen I could hear Ben's voice. I tried not to listen to what was being said; I didn't want to get depressed. I sought out the box that was on the top of the closet. Whoever raided us took only food and supplies, had hadn't looked in that closet. I grabbed two vials and a packaged syringe.

"Ben," I said softly. "How much of this euthanasia stuff will it take to put down a horse?"

"Oh my God," Ben replied, heartbroken. "What happened?"

"He was attacked by infected," Corbin answered. "He's pretty bad."

Corbin saw? Of course he did, that was what he kept trying to tell me but I wasn't listening.

"Nila," Ben said. "You can't give the horse that. You need to hit a vein and we don't have a syringe strong enough. You're gonna have to put him down another way."

A lump formed in my throat.

"Make sure you're close," Corbin added, "real close. About a foot. You don't want to miss. It would make things worse."

I cringed. "I'll try, then I'll be back for the kids." I remembered as I headed back out that my gun was by Lev. There was a rifle in the truck we always kept there and I went to get that.

How was I going to shoot Seltzer? It was going to be impossible.

Outside I could hear Seltzer groaning and crying. He was in agony. I got the rifle from Lev's truck, made sure it was loaded, clicked off the safety, and walked to Seltzer.

My hands trembled, my arm shook. I was an expert shot, but I was so fearful that my emotions were going to get the best of me and I would miss, causing Seltzer even more pain.

The poor horse had no reaction to me walking up to him. He wasn't jerking back when he saw me.

I knelt by his head, and stroked his mane. "I am so sorry, boy. Thank you for saving my life and getting me out of there. I am so sorry that this happened. I'm sorry about everything." I looked up to the sky.

How did we get here? How did we get to that point where there were more graves on the property than people alive? I was beginning to think it was only a matter of time until we all were gone. That maybe the living had their time on Earth, the human race did its damage, and now our time was up.

I gave a few more minutes to Seltzer, but I knew Ben needed to focus and concentrate on Lev and I had to get the three kids away.

I apologized once more and stood.

I walked behind him so he wouldn't see the rifle and I lowered it close to his head. The weapon swayed from my trembling hands. I tried my best to aim. Listening to his cries of pain told me it was something that needed to be done.

It was an act of mercy.

Inside I felt different. I felt horrible, guilt ridden and saddened. Still, as heartbreaking as it was, it had to be done.

"I'm sorry, boy."

I pulled the trigger.

SEVENTEEN

ICU

More than anything, I wanted to think clearly. Since the day my father died things had been relatively easy at the cabin. We were so secluded it was hard to believe that there was an insane world out there. When it came, it didn't just knock on our door, it burst in. A day that had started out pretty normal quickly cascaded into a nightmare. Kids tend to be resilient, and our three were dealing with things at such a young age that even we adults couldn't deal with. Billy and Sawyer were a little older than Katie, so they understood better.

Billy was doing the best. Maybe because he had already lost everyone close to him. Sawyer was still trying to understand that his grandmother had been killed, and Katie was worried about Lev.

When we met Corbin and his son, Sawyer's mother wasn't in the picture. It was a conversation we never had and I didn't know what had happened to her. It was a bad time to ask, and I went on the assumption she'd died in the outbreak.

The kids knew only a little more than I did.

According to Sawyer, after Ben yelled at Corbin to find me, they went into the cabin.

While Edi was making breakfast, Lev raced in, grabbed a rifle, told Edi that people were trying to get in, and opened the storage area in the floor.

"He told us not to come out until we heard you," Sawyer said. "When we were climbing in, there was a shot and I heard my grandma scream."

"Then what happened?" I asked.

"Lev shut the hatch," Sawyer said. "It was dark. I was scared and I heard all kinds of guns shooting. There was banging and stuff above our heads, but we didn't make a sound."

"I didn't cry, Mommy," Katie added. "I wanted to. I didn't cry at all."

"Good girl."

I stayed in the RV with the kids, waiting for word on Lev. I still didn't know how Edi was attacked and Lev was shot. Ben was in the outhouse, so I doubted he knew either.

After maybe an hour or so, Corbin came in to tell me Ben was done, to give him a few minutes then he'd talk to me. After embracing his son, Corbin went out and began the process of digging two more graves.

Ben was a lot longer than a few minutes, by at least two hours. He was cleaning the cabin and covering the bloodstained floor with a carpet.

He had also cleaned up himself, but was still wearing the same clothes. When he walked toward the RV, I made a mad dash his way to find out about Lev and he merely asked, "Can I change first? I promise I will be right back."

The wait was driving me nuts. The people who attacked us were still around. I didn't feel safe. Although I did my best to rig the front gate, I knew it wasn't going to hold.

Finally Ben came outside to join me.

"How is he?" I asked.

"Lev's a strong man. He lost a lot of blood. I gave him a transfusion using my blood. We have to wait and see if that will work," Ben explained. "I don't think he's going to die?"

I exhaled in relief and embraced him. "Thank you."

"But…he took a hit to the gut. It went straight through. The bullet to the arm was superficial as well. The one that concerns me is the leg. Fortunately for Lev, it was a .22 caliber and the bullet was still in the tibia. I removed it, was able to find the missing two pieces, and set the tibia. It needs to be stabilized with a cast of some kind. He'll never heal correctly without it."

"Easy solution. I need an hour tops," I said. "I can take Corbin, or go myself, to the animal hospital. It's not far at all and I don't think it was hit because it's off the beaten path."

"It's too dangerous," Ben said. "Not with those people out there."

"You think they're still out there? Maybe they merely raided us and left."

He shook his head.

"What happened here? How are you?" I noticed the butterfly sutures on his forehead.

"I'm damn lucky to be alive," he said. "When Corbin told me you went out alone, I didn't think much of it until I smelled the dead. He said you smelled it too and I sent him for you. I didn't want to tell Lev until after Corbin went out for you. I did, and got the reaction I expected. He was mad. Taking Seltzer out around the property fence is one thing. Going to the lake is a whole other ballgame."

"What happened?"

"Nila, honestly, it happened so fast. I had a couple of bites of breakfast, went to use the john. While I was in there, I heard commotion, then a gunshot, a scream. I opened up the outhouse door and two men came from the cabin. I pulled my gun and when I saw them aim at me, I slammed the outhouse door and a bullet seared right in, hit me here." He pointed to his head. "Grazed me, but it knocked me back and out. I came to when I heard Corbin screaming."

"They probably thought they killed you. Ben, they took everything."

"Not everything."

"Yeah, we still have the stuff under the floor."

"And the station wagon," Ben said. "Corbin has been hiding stuff in that. He didn't trust Scott."

I sighed. "Scott's missing."

Ben chuckled. "Scott isn't missing, Nila. Come on, *he* did this. Corbin wasn't crazy at all. Scott sent smoke signals, he led them here. Probably knew he had a week until his friends arrived. He went up there to wait and then they came here."

"This is unreal.".

"Nila!" Corbin called and came from around the back of the cabin. "Some lady on the radio, KA4? She's calling."

KA4, that was Helena.

"Tell her I'm coming." I ran for the cabin, and as soon as I stepped inside I saw Lev on the couch. He was still out and I paused to run my hand down his arm.

I was excited and relieved to hear from Helena. She knew what was going on out there. She also had told me once about a camp in Bedford, Ohio. Maybe we'd be safer joining others once Lev was better.

I grabbed the radio and called her name with relief. "Helena."

"Hey, there Sweet Pea, how's it going?"

"Oh my God, horrible. We got hit. We got hit bad. I think they used an infected as a diversion once they got in. They took everything we had, shot and killed our people. It was calculated."

"I'm sorry, Sweet Pea."

"Thank you."

"I'm sorry that you are still alive."

My heart took a nosedive to my gut and I could barely breathe. "W-what?"

"Yeah. I guess my scouting party figured if they hit early enough they'd get you all. They weren't supposed to really kill you, just take your stuff and tell you to leave. I got word that some guy fired first and, well, they had to defend themselves."

"You…*you* did this? *Why?*"

"We have nothing. We lost everything to a band of fellas and a horde of infected."

"Why didn't you say something? I would have helped you."

"No you wouldn't have. You have enough for your group to survive," Helena said. *"Then again, I didn't realize how much growth possibility you had down at your place. From what I hear, it can accommodate forty of us."*

"I never told you where we were."

"Didn't need to. You just told me your name. Aren't many Nila and Levons that are together. Scott heard, he knew."

I instantly went from shock to anger. Hearing Ben speculate about Scott was one thing, knowing for a fact was another.

"You're a nice lady, Sweet Pea," Helena said. *"Scott don't want you dead, so here's the deal. Me and the rest of my people will be arriving tomorrow afternoon. You be gone. You and what's left of your people, you leave. If you're gone, good. If not, we kill you. We have about forty of us. Don't believe me, just wait around to find out."*

"We have an injured man."

"Not my problem."

"Just take Big Bear. This is my home."

"Oh, we plan on taking Big Bear, in fact we have. We want your place and we don't trust you so close. I'm sure you aren't comfortable with us that close. That's it. Leave by tomorrow afternoon and you stay alive."

"If we agree to leave, you get your people to stay away from us until then."

"Deal. And don't try to destroy that property. We can see you."

She ended transmission. Enraged, furious, all the negative feelings swirled inside of me and I stood. I walked straight out the door to the RV, grabbed the binoculars that hung from the back then, climbed to the top.

Across a small field began a long semi-steep slope. At the top was the back section of Big Bear, the area where the longtime campers like Edi and her husband stayed. I peered to the top of that hill. I could see figures. I lifted the binoculars. They must have known she was radioing because eight of them stood there. One even had the audacity to wave.

Eight of them.

I needed to come up with a plan. I couldn't give up my home without a fight. But even if Helena exaggerated about how many were in her group, we were outnumbered. With our strongest man down, how could we defeat those odds?

EIGHTEEN

LIGHT BULB

In my favorite spot on the top step of the front porch, I finished a cigarette and flicked the butt out to the grass. I took a sip of bourbon and lit another. I was looking for something, anything to calm me down. Truth was, I hadn't had a cigarette in a long time. Actually, I had not had one since that night when I drove off with my drunken friends. Lev had taken them from my hand and the one from my mouth, and said, 'You are not the bad girl, Nila. Stop trying to be.'

In the aftermath of all that happened, I wanted so much to be that bad girl. To be the type of person whose anger and rage fueled the courage to do something and stand by my convictions. Instead, I was far from it. My anger fueled fear, worry, and perhaps cowardice. I was confused and bitter because I needed Lev. Not to protect me, but help me figure out what to do. It was easy for Ben and Corbin since this wasn't their home, their land, or a cabin that their father had built with his own hands. This was mine. And someone wanted it. No, they didn't just want. They were going to *take* it, with force if need be.

It killed me to see Lev so weak. To make matters worse his leg truly needed to be set in some sort of cast or medical splint. On top of that, we had to move him. Ben said there was nothing we could do.

Fuck that.

"Nila, I will make a splint out of wood. We'll make it work for now."

"Wouldn't it be better if we set it permanently?" I asked.

"Would it be best to set it properly before we move him? Yes. But there's nothing we can do. We don't have a choice in the matter."

"Yes, we do."

"At what cost? Your life? No."

Again, fuck that.

I made the decision to take the truck and head down to that veterinarian clinic. It wasn't that far. They would have what we needed. They would have the plaster, the bandages, whatever it took.

"Make me a list." I said to Ben.

"I can't believe you're going to do this. Think about your daughter. What would she do if something happened to you?" Ben tried to persuade me.

"Nothing is going to happen. I'm heading straight there. I can outrun the dead, and I'll plow through any infected. I've been down there. There's not that many. I can make it there and back in less than an hour."

"What about those men on the hill?"

"Helena said they'd leave us alone."

Ben snorted. "Really? You're trusting the word of the people that robbed you? Raided your home? Killed our people?"

"What choice do I have?"

"Stay. Let me make a splint. A temporary one that will work well enough for us to move him."

I thought about it for moment, and then simply said, "Please keep an eye on my daughter. This camp will be safe."

It was stupid, yes, but it was something I had to do. Admittedly, I was glad Corbin came with me. He and I took Lev's truck, secured the gate after we pulled through, went down to the main road, and headed to the veterinarian hospital.

"They're going to follow us," said Corbin.

"You think?"

"Yeah. Especially if they see one truck leaving and other people left behind."

He had a point. I kept looking in the rearview mirror.

There were two things on the way to the veterinarian hospital, that surprised me. One, they didn't follow us. I admit that the prospect of them tailing us made me a little frightened. What would they do with us? Would they kill us as well? The other thing that surprised me was the amount of infected. There weren't hordes of them, but there were a lot. A minimal amount of infected, small groups of five or six, staggered about the road running after us as we went by them. I had to wonder if these people, the ones that hit our camp, had brought the infected. Maybe led them to us as some sort of offensive move.

I was alone with Corbin for the first time. Away from all the craziness, I realized I hadn't said anything to him. We were so consumed by all that happened I hadn't mentioned the fact that he lost his mother.

"I'm sorry about your mother," I said. "That was tragic. She was a wonderful person and didn't deserve that."

I looked over to him and he was staring out the window.

Corbin cleared his throat and looked at me, "Thank you for that."

A few more moments of silence passed.

"I never asked about your wife, Sawyer's mom," I said. "If it's too painful to talk about, I understand. I was just curious."

"We weren't married. Sawyer's mom died before all this craziness, when Sawyer was two years old. She was an addict. She OD'd when he was with her. I was at work when I got the call. My son was alone for hours. It's probably why I am so anti-drug now," he said. "Me, my mom, and my dad were all he had in this world. Now they're gone. I have to be there for him. You know that feeling. You're in the same position."

I was. I also wondered if I didn't have Katie, would I be bowing out and leaving my home so easily?

There had to be a solution. How could someone just strong arm us like that and get away with it? It was a new world, with new rules.

We arrived at the hospital, and as I suspected, it was so far away from anything that we didn't see a single infected. It looked exactly as Cade and I left it months earlier. I suspected it hadn't been touched.

After parking the truck, I stepped out and looked around.

"We need to make it fast in case they do come looking for us," I said and opened the back door that Cade and I had used previously.

"Is there anything left?" Corbin asked. "Didn't you and Brian wipe it out?"

"No, we took only what we needed," I said. "Check the rooms. See if you see plaster bandages, anything with the word plaster. That's what Ben said we needed. I'll check the storeroom."

"I'll look for the operating room. Usually vets store stuff in there."

I went into the storeroom. As soon as I stepped inside I thought about Cade and how he'd known exactly what to look for. I had a list from Ben. It was short. The bandages, antibiotics, I knew where to get. Cade had shown me before.

My mind was beyond full. I thought of Cade, of Lev, of the cabin, and how many memories were made there. Why couldn't I fix it? Why couldn't I figure out a way?

I grabbed things I suspected would work. Corbin returned not long after he started searching, he had found the plaster bandages. We grabbed a ton, figuring with kids, we might need it again.

When we finished and were gathering all that we could, I saw a locked cabinet with a glass front. Behind lock and key I saw bottles of apomorphine. My husband Paul was allergic to dogs, but before marrying him, I had a dog all my life. I wasn't sure what apomorphine was used for exactly in humans, but I knew why the vet had it, and that gave me an idea of what I needed to do.

NINETEEN

FROM LEV'S SIDE

I thought I had died.

There was never a time in my life when I doubted the existence of God and Heaven, so when I was face to face with my father, who had passed away months earlier, I knew for certain I didn't live through that attack.

"Hang in there, Lev, hang in there. You're doing good," my father said.

"Thanks."

"Almost there. Just hang on."

Then I realized that I hadn't died and it may have looked like my father, but it was a dream and the voice was Ben's.

I drifted in and out of consciousness a lot as he worked on me, never fully wakening enough to respond, always falling back into some sort of dream. Daggers of horrendous pain would shoot through me, causing me to jolt awake. I never registered it completely.

I had survived and I felt emotionally destroyed.

The night before it all happened I was talking to Nila, laying across the foot of her bed. I was so tired that I was nodding off while talking and said nonsense several times. She laughed at me and I finally passed out.

When I woke up she was gone, and I heard some sort of heated discussion between Ben and Corbin. I didn't think much about it, they argued a lot. Katie was in the kitchen with Edi. She had made some homemade biscuits and sent Katie to get the other kids.

When the three of them came into the cabin, I noticed Corbin had taken the truck. My first thought was that he was going fishing. A few minutes later, probably enough time for Corbin to make it down the driveway, Ben came in.

"What's going on?" I asked. 'I heard you arguing."

"Nila left on Seltzer," Ben said. "I sent Corbin after her."

"Why? She always takes Seltzer around the property."

"She went looking for Scott."

"Where did he go?" I asked.

"He told Corbin fishing, but I don't trust that. I don't trust him at all. That wasn't the reason I sent Corbin. There's a smell of death out there. Infected are close."

When I started to charge for the door Ben blocked me. "Give him time to get her. She'll be fine. Give it a couple minutes. Let me hit the john, then if you still want to go out, we'll go uncover the station wagon." Ben was calm about it, confident, and even stole a biscuit before going out the back door.

I wasn't so calm. With my coffee, I went outside to keep an eye out. After only a minute, I saw Scott at the gate. My first thought was that Ben was wrong, Scott was fine, and Nila would be back. As I lifted my hand to wave, two cars pulled up and seven men got out. One of the men tugged a woman from the car. She had a hood over her head, covering her face. I thought it was Nila, that they had gotten her.

Every one of those men were armed, and when they lifted the hood off of the woman, I saw it wasn't Nila, but an infected. Dropping my coffee, I barreled into the house, and lifted the hatch to the floorboard storage.

"Edi, go get Ben, then get in your trailer. We have people trying to get in." I grabbed Katie and carried her to the storage. "Boys. In. Now."

"Why, Lev, what's going on?" Katie asked.

"Down. Now," I ordered. "It will be tight but stay here, all of you." The boys climbed in. "Don't make a noise. Stay in there until you hear me or Nila tell you it's safe."

I remembered their scared faces as they crowded in the storage area staring up at me.

A shot rang out and Sue Ellen screamed.

"Stay!" I ordered. I slammed the hatch, tossed the rug over it, engaged the rifle, and walked outside. I could have stayed in the cabin, shot from the window. I didn't want to fire the gun around the kids in case they screamed.

The second I stepped out, the first bullet hit my arm at the same time I saw them gun down Sue Ellen.

I got off maybe two shots when a second bullet hit my shin, breaking my leg, and I went down.

The door was still open and all I could think about was making sure they didn't find those kids. I lifted myself to stand, tried to turn, and another shot hit me in the gut.

My knees buckled, my leg wouldn't move, and I staggered into the living room. Edi's screams carried in from outside. I couldn't do anything. My goal was the carpet that covered the hatch. I knew I was falling, I couldn't walk, but I had to get there.

Giving it all I had, four good steps, I arrived and toppled to the floor. At the very least the kids were hidden beneath me, they were safe.

The men rampaged through the cabin, calling out, 'get this, get that, hurry'. I knew Scott and the men were taking everything we had. In my mind I begged, *Please, Nila stay away until they are gone.*

Sometime during it all I lost consciousness and didn't regain any of it until I heard Ben's voice within the dream of my father.

Whatever pain I felt paled in comparison to the pain of my emotions. I'd failed. I had the single task of protecting the cabin and those in it and I failed.

Sue Ellen was dead. Edi was screaming. Before that she had barely made a noise above a whisper, yet her cries were screeching and filled with pain and fear.

For the longest time I didn't know if Nila or the kids were alive or dead. I hadn't heard them at all.

Then after another round of unconsciousness, I woke to hear her voice.

My eyes were heavy. I tried to open them, to talk. I couldn't do either.

"Any problems?" Ben asked.

"No. None," Nila said. "Corbin and I were in and out. We got some other stuff too, if you want to take a look."

"I will. Right now, I need to set that leg."

"What do you need me to do?" Nila asked.

"Nothing. Just stay with the kids. I'll let you know when I'm done."

The kids.

They were all right.

I heard Nila leave and that was the moment I was able to make a noise. I grunted in pain.

"Hey there, Lev," Ben said. "I'm setting your leg."

I opened my eyes and tried to focus.

"There you are," Ben said. "Good to see you up. Unfortunately, I have to set your leg, so I'm gonna have to knock you out again." He lifted a syringe and leaned over me. "When you wake up, you'll feel better."

My whole body was in pain so I didn't even know if he gave me the injection. I do know I passed out again. When I started to come to, I heard Nila's voice.

"Will he wake up?" she asked.

"Of course," Ben replied. "Nila, I'm worried about you. You need to stay out of the woods."

Why was Nila in the woods?

"I was checking on things. Making sure."

"Yeah, well, leave that to Corbin please," Ben said.

"Why? Because he's a man?"

"No, there's other reasons."

"Will he remember?" Nila asked.

"Who?"

"Lev. When he wakes up, will he have amnesia?"

Ben laughed. "Nila, he didn't hit his head."

"We don't know."

"No, we don't. But I didn't see any signs of that."

"Were you looking?"

"Nila..."

"Sorry. Is he going to be all right to move tomorrow?"

Move? Where are they moving me?

When I heard that I struggled to wake up. My eyes were heavy, like they were stuck to my eyeballs and couldn't move.

"I hope," Ben said. "I don't want him walking. Not with the stomach wound. It won't be easy for him. I'd like him to stay flat but he's a big guy, heavy too. Corbin and I had a tough time getting him from the floor to the couch."

"Maybe if we make a gurney," Nila said. "He has to be, like, three hundred pounds."

What! I do not weigh that much!

I had to get my eyes open, say something. If I didn't she would tell the story of my youth and weight issues.

"When he was a kid, he used to be—"

"Nila," I groaned.

"There he is," Ben said.

"Lev!" She hurried to my side, lowering down to be close. "Hey. How are you?"

"Sore," I said groggily. "I'll get better."

"I know you will." She held my hand.

"I'll leave you two be," Ben said. "I'll be back in an hour to check on you."

After he was gone, Nila said, "He did so good for a plastic surgeon. We're lucky you're alive."

"I'm sorry."

"For?" she asked.

"I am so sorry I failed. I believed Scott, I trusted him. Sue Ellen is dead. I don't know about Edi…"

Nila shook her head. "They brought an infected. It got her. They shot at Ben, but he lived obviously."

"I failed."

117

"Are you fucking kidding me?" she asked. "Lev, Katie, Sawyer, and Billy are alive because of you. This attack was coming no matter what. Scott was with Helena's camp."

"Helena?"

"Yeah, he heard our names. That's how he knew where to go. I'm guessing the smoke signal was to let them know the camp was clear."

"So Helena and her people are at Big Bear?"

"Not yet. Tomorrow, and they want us out. They took everything except what was in the floorboard spaces and anything they thought was part of the cabin, and they said they have a large group. We go or we die."

I closed my eyes. "What are we going to do?"

"We don't have the manpower to fight them. We have kids. We go," she said. "I don't want to leave my home, but leaving for now is the only choice."

"For now? You mean for good."

"You never know."

"Where are we going to go? Do you have any ideas?"

"Yeah, I do. You need to rest, 'cause I need you Lev. I really need you." She leaned forward and placed her lips to my forehead. "We have a long road ahead of us and I'll be damned if I am going to take it without you."

"I'll do my best."

She smiled. "You always do."

"Nila? There's something I need to tell you."

"Yes?"

I squeezed her hand. "I don't weigh three hundred pounds."

She laughed and placed her forehead against mine. I knew at that moment, no matter what was ahead, we would conquer it.

TWENTY

SKILL SET

August 11

It was time to go. We didn't want to take any chances of Helena and her people showing up before we left. I had spent the entire night getting ready and packing my entire life and memories in boxes.

I also spent a good bit of the night angry. It was different when leaving was my idea, when Lev and I tried to get everyone to a Green Area. Now we were being forced out and I hated it. I hated them.

There were things hidden within the house, like food and Lisa's booze stash. Everything in both RVs except the chickens was there, so packing took a while.

Surprisingly, there were a lot of things they didn't take, either because they didn't know what they were, thought they were part of the house, or planned on coming back. The solar generator was one of them and I was grateful for that. It was one of the heaviest items to move.

The other was Lev.

I was super impressed when Corbin pulled out the Flex Flyer Sled from the shed. I had forgotten about that. It was old and rusty and a part of my past. As kids, Lev and I took that sled down the big hill between my cabin and Big Bear more times than we could count, each time getting in trouble. Lev was such a solid kid, that sled moved fast and never flipped.

We used it to move a lot of items. Corbin wanted to use it to move Lev. I was high fiving and praising him until Ben slapped that idea down.

"Just back the truck up to the porch and we'll carry him the ten feet," Ben said.

There was no way Lev could ride passenger, not with his stomach wound and broken leg. So it was decided that Corbin would drive the station wagon with his son and Ben would drive the truck with Katie and Billy up front while I rode in the back with Lev.

It was fast approaching time to go, and Corbin still had to get the station wagon from its hidden spot. I went to get him and found him by the graves, just standing there.

"When I left before with Lev," I said as I approached, "walking away from this cemetery was the hardest part. I hated the thought of leaving my father."

"So many graves," Corbin said.

"Yeah, there are. Too many."

"It's not hard to leave now?" he asked.

"No, we'll be back."

"You sound so sure."

"I am. We'll be back. I promise you. At least to get our stuff."

He gave me a quizzical look as if waiting for more of an explanation.

"We have to go." When I turned I saw the door to the shed where we kept Lester was open. "Oh shit."

"What?"

"The shed is open."

"Yep." Corbin nodded.

"Did he die?"

"No. He's gone."

"What happened? Did he escape? I asked.

"Don't worry about it." Corbin kissed his hand then touched it to his mother's grave. "I'm ready."

"Corbin, did you set him free on purpose?"

"All's fair in love in war, right?" he asked and started walking. "They brought one here, it's only right we return the favor."

"You took him to Big Bear," I said giddily. "When?"

"I took him close enough to get a scent about an hour ago. You know," he raised an eyebrow, "when you were busy doing…things."

"What was that look about?"

"Nothing. Do you miss gravy at all?"

"Yeah," I chuckled. "Corbin, how did you get him there?"

"Gotta love that sled."

"Yeah, you do."

"You guys drop me off near the end of the driveway and I'll get the station wagon. We can stop down the road and switch up."

"Sounds good." I walked to the truck.

Ben stood by it, waiting. "Do we know where we're headed?"

"We need to plan," I said. "For the short term, I have an idea."

I climbed in the back of the truck with Lev, as did Corbin, and we pulled away from the property. I watched from the back of the truck as I left the cabin like when we left weeks earlier.

Only this time I was certain, like I had told Corbin, we would be back.

We didn't pass any of Helena's people or a caravan of forty. We did, however, pass an unusual amount of infected and dead on the road. Some of the dead crawled with their last ounce of energy, limbs dragging behind them.

Were they brought here or had they migrated?

Whatever the case, it made me start to wonder if we were on round two or three of the outbreak. Would there ever be a pause or an end where it was just us in a dead world?

Spending a lot of time in this rural backwoods area gave me the advantage of knowing what was around and what was close.

We needed a plan and we needed a place where we could give Lev time to regain his strength. As much as he wanted to portray he was on a fast track to recovery, I knew he wasn't. Lev was pale and slightly warm from fever. Travelling aimlessly to find a new home was out of the question.

Though Ben insisted we shoot straight for Canada, even he didn't want to be on the road with Lev yet.

Knowing the area, I knew where we could go. It was about eighteen miles south, a thirty minute drive. One Bobby and I had made numerous times once we were legally old enough to drink.

There was never a shortage of bars in the area but he and I favored the Windhaven.

It wasn't far from Evans City, on a road that transformed from a four-lane major thoroughfare to a two-lane road, from a bustling area to a rural one.

The Windhaven had a frame structure with beat up white siding and plenty of room to move. It wasn't exceptionally large but it was big enough. I used to call it a firetrap because the first floor had only two doors and not a single window. There looked to be an apartment above it, however, I'd never been inside of it.

The lack of windows and entrance as well as how far removed it was made it the ideal location to wait out Lev's recovery. We could have found a house, but the Windhaven was more solid and a safer place than a house or business with windows that could be broken.

I expected the Windhaven to be like the veterinary hospital, isolated and untouched. I didn't expect when we approached it to see a swarm of infected not just around the building, but hitting against the siding and doors, trying to get in.

We stopped far enough away and off the road to see, out of sight and smell of the infected.

Corbin pulled the station wagon right behind us. Lev tried to sit up and I stopped him.

"What's happening?" he asked.

"Get this, there's like twenty or so infected hitting the Windhaven like in *Night of the Living Dead*."

Katie peered through the truck window and waved to me, unfazed by what was happening.

I returned the wave as both Ben and Corbin walked up to the back of the truck, none of us really taking our eyes from the infected.

"Now what?" Ben asked.

"This is unbelievable," I said. "We didn't see a single infected for miles now. Then we get here." I held out my hand, palm up, in the direction of the Windhaven. "What the hell? This is, like, in the middle of nowhere."

Corbin scratched his head. "We can turn around. I saw a garage about a mile back."

"No," Ben answered. "Problem with that is it's too close to the infected. We can keep moving, but honestly, we need to get Lev somewhere stable."

"Why are they there?" I asked.

"One of two reasons," Ben replied. "Either they are working on instinct and memory like you theorize and they all came here out of habit."

"Like they're all Friday night regulars?" Corbin asked.

"Aw, see," I pouted. "You're making fun of my theory. They're still alive, so they're still human. Somewhere in there is a consciousness or memory that comes out."

"I'm sure." Ben nodded. "Or they're chasing a scent."

"You think someone's in there?" I asked. "I don't see a truck or car."

"They could be trapped," Ben said. "No windows. No way to shoot them, and no way to get a clear shot from that second floor. They can either go out and kill them or wait it out.

I stared out toward the Windhaven where the infected were still oblivious to us. They clearly wanted in that building.

"You can pull the cars back. I'm a pretty good shot. I get a little closer and stay hidden, I probably could take them out," I said.

"What about noise?" Ben asked. "There's about twenty or twenty-five. Even if you hit each one precisely with one shot, we're still talking twenty shots going off. It'll call more infected if they're in the area. Not to mention if Helena's people are anywhere nearby, they'll hear us."

I shrugged. "Then I guess we find someplace else."

"That's the logical thing, but if there are people in there, they can use some help," Ben said.

"You said no shooting," I replied.

"There are other places," Lev said. "Let's just go."

"You're right," Ben said. "Let's head out." He looked at the Windhaven. "We have supplies. We just need shelter." He started walking back to the driver's door and I positioned myself next to Lev in the back.

"Wait," Corbin called out and pointed. "Look."

I turned around. From the side window of the second floor apartment, we saw a waving towel. Someone was flagging us.

Ben was right, they needed help.

More than likely, as he suggested, there weren't enough people inside to fight off the infected and or they didn't have the weapons to do so.

I stood up with my rifle. "I'll go take the side—"

"No. No shooting. It's a bad idea." Ben looked at Corbin. "You did it before. You up for it again?'

"Did what before?" I asked.

Corbin exhaled. "Yeah. I'll handle it."

"What? He'll handle what?"

Corbin walked back to the station wagon, reached in behind the driver's seat, and returned with a red and black gun-like object. It was obvious that there were some adjustments to the chamber, but it was clearly a nail gun.

"Oh my God," I said. "For real?"

"What?" Corbin asked. "I got heavy duty wood to steel two-inchers in here. It's pneumatic. Powerful."

"Yeah, I get it. You want to fire it on the group of infected so you don't make any noise. That doesn't work. In the movies it does, not in real life."

"It does," Corbin argued.

"No it doesn't. Tell him, Lev," I said. "Nailers don't work like they do in the movies as weapons."

"They bounce," Lev said.

"They do bounce," I said. "Trust me, we tried it as kids. Even on cardboard, they bounce. They got a good velocity but they don't penetrate from any distance."

"Hell, I know that," Corbin scoffed. "Everyone does. That's not how it's done." He then proceeded to walk toward the Windhaven.

I wanted to scream, shriek for him to stop, but I was afraid to draw their attention. "Ben," I said through clenched teeth, "he is getting too close."

"I know."

"It's suicide."

"No, he has a...a special skill."

"Skill with a nailer or not, it's suicide, there's too many." I jumped from the back of the truck with my rifle.

"Nila," Ben held out his arm to stop me.

"Get ready to pull out fast." I pushed past. It was insane. Corbin got closer and closer. The infected would notice him and rage toward him, he wouldn't have a chance. All I saw in my mind was Corbin being torn to shreds in front of his son.

Close enough to get a good shot, I stopped, got a good stance, and raised my weapon. My plan was to pick off the ones closest to Corbin first. I watched where he walked and got one in my scope. I didn't want to pull the trigger until Corbin was there. One shot. One noise. That close, Corbin was done.

Or so I thought.

It didn't dawn on me to question how he was getting so close without being seen. It should have.

The moment I was about to press the trigger, Corbin walked up behind an infected woman, lifted the nailer to the back of her neck near the base of the skull, and fired.

The infected went down and Corbin quickly moved to the next, doing the same thing. At first I attributed it to his coming up from behind; they didn't sense, see, or smell him. Then he pulled one from the door, 'nailed' him, and grabbed another.

They weren't reacting to him. They weren't attacking. They focused on the Windhaven without a clue that Corbin was among them playing executioner. They'd get hit and merely drop.

Although I kept my rifle raised just in case, there was no need. Corbin was cutting through the infected and it shocked the hell out of me. When Ben said Corbin had a special skill, he wasn't kidding. I just couldn't fathom what made him so special.

TWENTY-ONE

THE CHOICE

There were so many questions I had about Corbin in the seconds following him clearing the area. He turned around in the middle of the carnage and looked at me. Not with a look of 'hey, I'm cool', but rather, 'I did what needed to be done'.

Corbin was winded, his shoulders drooped, and his face was pale. It took a lot out of him to do that. He concentrated and got the job done.

But how?

Had it been me, they would have engulfed me.

I lowered my rifle, frozen in my stance, ready to say something when the windowless white metal front door of the Windhaven was flung open and a tall man wearing faded jeans, a dirty tee shirt, and a bandana, appeared.

"Help, can you help, please?" he said frantically. "Please! Help!"

He left the door as fast as he appeared, leaving it open.

"Go drive the wagon." Corbin didn't wait for my reply before he ran in.

Was he nuts? He was just going to run in there on the pleas of a stranger? It could have been a trap. I signaled to Ben that I was going in as well, and I imagine he thought the same as me because he threw up his hands, almost as if asking what I was thinking.

When I ran inside, I couldn't see Corbin.

The Windhaven was sectioned off by a semi open wall. On one side was a large bar, the other had tables and a dance floor.

I didn't get a chance to notice what all remained, or if it was disheveled. I was looking for Corbin. The Windhaven wasn't that big, I should have been able to see him.

"Corbin!"

I didn't hear him, but I heard something else, a woman. She was screaming and it sounded as if she was in pain.

"Corbin!"

"Nila!" he shouted in the distance. "Up here!"

I followed the sound of his voice to a door next to the kitchen behind the bar. It was open and there was a staircase.

Just as I lifted my foot to the first step, Corbin called out again. "Nila, go get Ben. Get him now! Hurry!"

He sounded as frantic as the man who opened the door. I ran and got Ben.

If it was urgent that I get Ben, that could only mean one thing…a medical emergency. Lev being incapacitated would leave the kids vulnerable if I too went to see what was going on so I stayed behind. I brought Sawyer into the truck and drove it behind The Windhaven to the back door. After I got the kids inside, unfortunately with Lev still in the bed of the truck, I ran back and got the station wagon.

I stayed at the back of the truck, near the door, keeping an eye on the kids while watching Lev.

Corbin soon came back down.

"What's going on?" I asked.

"Let's get Lev inside and secure this place."

"Corbin, what the hell?"

"Please. Ben needs a few minutes, then wants you up there."

"Me?"

"Yeah, you."

"Why?"

"You'll see. Before you go up, I need help with Lev."

"This is ridiculous," Lev said. "I'll walk." With a groan and his face wincing from the pain, he partially sat up.

"Lev, stop!" I shrieked.

"No, I'm not going to stop, Nila. I'll get in there and then rest again. Okay?" He looked at me. "I am not going to have you carry me. The bullet hit nothing but flesh and muscle."

"He's got a point." Corbin nodded at Lev.

"He's got a cast. He can't walk on that."

"He can lean on us," Corbin said then turned to Lev. "Will that work?"

Lev laughed at that notion and sniffed. "Yeah, that will work."

The Windhaven had thick wooden tables and we put two together against a wall, placed the cot mattress on them, and made Lev a bed. It would have to do, although I didn't see Lev staying down for very long. Ben promised if Lev rested his leg for five days, he'd replace the cast with something easier, even though it could mean slower healing. In a world with fast running infected Lev needed to be more mobile.

I felt bad for several reasons. Lev being injured for one, and another that the poor kids were sitting in chairs, looking lost and not knowing what to do.

Once we got Lev settled, Corbin said he was going to unload the truck, and I went upstairs. I heard him telling the kids it was all right if they played with the balls on the pool table as long as they didn't throw them at each other.

At the top of the staircase I stopped hearing the kids and heard something else, moans of pain and crying.

131

Like when I first entered the Windhaven, it was a woman and it hit me, the sounds she was making were from being in labor. Ben was delivering a baby.

The guy who had opened the door stood outside the room at the end of the hall, one arm wrapped across his waist, his other hand covering his face.

"Is that your wife in there?" I asked.

He shook his head. "A friend."

As I turned to walk in, a young girl, a teenager, barreled out, nearly knocking me over. At the same time a long, loud scream emerged.

I expected to walk in to a woman bearing down, I didn't expect to walk in to blood.

The bed was saturated with it, creating a huge circle around the woman. It had soaked through the sheet that covered her.

Ben was bent over at the side of the bed looking desperate. It was obvious he was trying to listen to her stomach with the stethoscope. The woman wasn't having it.

"Christina, listen to me," Ben said calmly. "I have to listen, okay? So you have to be quiet."

"It hurts!" she cried.

"I know," Ben said softly. "This is not normal. I need to move fast for you and the baby." He glanced at me. "Can you help, Nila, please?"

Help? What was I supposed to do? I walked over to the bed. "Christina, I'm Nila. Is this your first baby?"

What was I thinking? What kind of question was that? Even if it was her first baby, she knew something was wrong.

She grabbed my hand desperately, her hands slick with blood, and pulled her face closer to mine. "Don't let my baby die. Please don't let my baby die. He's all I have left. Don't let my baby die!" She begged.

"Nila." Ben waved me over to the end of the bed.

"I don't know what you need me to do. I don't know any of this. Corbin probably could help."

"Medically yeah, he could," Ben said. "Emotionally, statistics show if there is another woman in the room, it helps. I need her calm."

"She's in labor, right?"

"No. She's not. She's in pain, but not dilated, and her abdomen is soft."

I didn't know what that meant.

"She suffered a trauma to her stomach yesterday morning. Pain started about an hour ago and she's bleeding out."

"The placenta separated."

"Placenta abruption from trauma, the worst kind. We're probably already too late. If I have an inkling of saving her, I have to take the baby now. I have a faint heartbeat, but any longer and the baby will die. If we leave the baby in she'll die. In fact, to do this, I have to put her under. I have morphine. That might kill her. She may die anyhow from blood loss or cardiac arrest."

"Be honest, *is* she going to die anyhow?" I asked.

"I don't know. More than likely. There is a chance I can save her, a slim chance."

I folded my arms tight against my body. I understood his dilemma. Should he fight for the mother's life at the risk of the baby's when her chances of death were greater?

It was a shit world, a horrible world. "What about making her comfortable and letting them both pass?" I suggested.

"That's another option. One I don't like. I think we should try to save a life. I won't make the call to put them down."

"Sometimes there are circumstances that we don't have any choice over and the outcome is the same. Like putting down a loved one sick with the virus."

"We think that," Ben argued, "but we don't know. We think it will go one way and it goes the other. If I went the correct route with Corbin he'd be dead. He's not."

That confused me. Apparently something happened with him.

"Did Corbin make that call?" I asked.

"No, I did."

"Then do the same here."

Ben took a deep breath and moved to his bag. He began removing items, including morphine and surgical tools in a sealed hospital bag.

Figuring she needed to be calm and told what was happening, I walked back to the bed. Christina was hyperventilating from crying.

"Christina," I said calmly, "the accident that hurt you caused the placenta to detach. You're bleeding really bad, you know that." I swept her curly brown hair from her eyes and drew myself close to her. I took a moment to think what I would say, how I would say it. I had to be honest with her if she was going to make the choice. "Things aren't good. Ben is a good doctor. He's going to give you something to relax you and he's going to remove the baby and try to save you both."

She gripped my hand so tight. I saw the alarm in her eyes, she thought only the baby was in danger. She didn't realize how bad she was. "Could I die?"

I looked up at Ben.

"We're going to do all we can," he answered. "I will try my hard-est."

"Is there…is there a chance the baby lives and I die?" she asked.

"I'm gonna try to not let that happen," Ben explained. "I'll take the baby and will have to perform a hysterectomy. I have to do so now."

Surprising me, Christina shook her head frantically. Her eyes rolled slightly out of control when she did. "Then no. No. I can't...I can't take that chance. I can't have him live without me. If I won't live to protect him, let us go."

"Are you sure?" I asked.

Christina nodded.

Ben was prepping her stomach and I reached up and stopped him.

"She doesn't want it," I said. "Give her the morphine and let her rest."

I wanted to ask her again, to double check that it was what she wanted. My attention was away from her only a second, but that was all it took. A second. "Christina, just to..." Her grip loosened, her head slumped to the side, her wide open, eyes stared blankly out.

My lungs filled with a burning air that made it hard for me to exhale. I blinked long and hard, absorbing what happened.

Another death.

I didn't know why, but I instantly grieved her. I felt her pain, her hard choice as a mother.

"Ben, she's gone," I whispered.

Her pinky finger was still semi latched onto my hand and gently I pulled her hand away, resting it on the bed. I reached up and closed her eyes, whispering, "I'm sorry."

When I stood, Ben hurriedly brought the scalpel to her stomach.

"Oh my God, what are you doing?"

"Removing the baby."

"Ben..."

"He's still alive. He won't be in a minute."

"You can't do this. She didn't want—"

"You told me to make the call, did you not?" Ben asked, furiously working.

"Yes, but—"

"I'm making the call. I can't, Nila. I can't let this baby die without trying. Can you get me a towel, or blanket?"

Was he even thinking it through, beyond the birth? I left the room to find him a blanket or towel. I was shocked at his decision, but with each second that passed after Christina's death, I understood it.

TWENTY-TWO

BACK STORY

I was emotionally and physically burned out when I returned downstairs. Ben stayed upstairs with the baby. He wasn't premature, at least I didn't think. He was average size. I believe that was one of the reasons Ben wanted to save him. If born alive, he stood a chance at life. However, with things the way they were, that still remained to be seen.

I didn't know anything medical, only what Ben told me. He said it was a wait and see situation.

Truth be known, I could wait, but I didn't want to see.

I was so tired of death. Finished with it. But it wasn't the end and I was sure I would see so much more.

The stranger who asked us for help was still in the hallway. I said, "I'm sorry," as I passed him.

At the bottom of the stairs, I heard Lev talking to the kids. They were giggling and it was good to hear.

Early in the day or not, I needed a drink. Before stepping behind the bar, I glanced into the bigger room. The back door was closed, and Corbin seemed to be organizing supplies. I couldn't see Lev, he was against the wall, but I could see the kids sitting in chairs in front of him.

The bar was still fully stocked, the three residents obviously weren't big drinkers. Then again, I didn't know how long they had been taking refuge in the Windhaven.

I grabbed a bottle of whiskey. It didn't matter what brand. I dusted off a glass from the bar and poured a healthy drink.

"Are they dead?" I heard a meek voice ask.

I took a drink and looked behind me. The teenage girl sat at the far corner of the bar, eating from one of those bar size bags of chips. Her hair was pulled in a loose ponytail, her face puffy from crying, and there was an abrasion on her cheek.

"When did you eat last?" I asked.

"This morning I had pretzels. Are they dead?"

I took another drink.

"I'll assume they are."

I shook my head. "Christina died. I'm sorry."

Her eyes widened. "The baby is still alive?"

The moment I said, "Yes," she jumped up. I stopped her. "Ben is still working up there. Give him a few more minutes."

She slid back down on to the barstool.

"What's your name?" I asked.

"Bella."

"Bella, that's a beautiful name. How old are you?"

"How old are you?" Bella snapped. "What's with all the questions?"

"I'm just trying to get to know you."

"Well don't, okay? I'm tired of getting to know people and then they die." She shoved a chip in her mouth and chomped hard.

"I hear you." I finished my drink.

After a few seconds of silence between us, with Lev and the kids' voices in the background, she said, "I knew her the longest."

I poured some more whisky in my glass, then looked at her, letting her know she had my attention.

"We met right after the outbreak," Bella said. "I lost my mom and dad, she lost her family. We had been travelling together a few weeks when we met up with Fleck and the gang." She pointed up. "Fleck is the guy upstairs."

I nodded. "So they aren't family?"

"Not blood. But in this world now, you become family pretty fast."

She was right. Strangers became people you held on to, and quickly too. My attention was drawn away when the kids laughed.

"Did you guys all meet up on the road?" Bella asked.

"Not all. The little girl is my daughter and the guy in there on the table has been my best friend since we were ten."

"You're lucky."

"Yeah, yeah, I am."

"I'm sorry I snapped at you. I'm fourteen."

I gave her a gentle smile. "It's okay, I understand. But don't expect me to tell you my age." I winked.

"Did you find the others on the road?"

"They found us. We were pretty safe and settled at my father's cabin. We had all we needed."

"Why did you leave?" she asked.

"You could say we didn't have a choice." I brought my drink to my lips. "But we'll go back. We'll get our stuff back. I'm sure of it."

Again, laughter caught my attention. What was he telling them?

"So don't let her tell you otherwise," Lev said. His voice was hoarse. "She didn't comb her hair right and your pap cut it off. She was twelve."

"That's not true!" I hollered his way. "You forgot he cut my hair off after Belinda already cut it during social studies."

"Oh yeah, that's right," Lev said.

"Is that true?" Bella asked.

"Yep." I raised my eyebrows. "She was a bully and she sat behind me. Cut off a big section of my long hair. I walked around all morning without noticing until kids started making fun of me at lunch."

"That's terrible. What did you do?"

"Nothing. I was a scared, timid girl. Revenge was a fantasy, not my strong point at that time. I didn't have it in me."

"What about now?"

I paused in answering, contemplated that question, took a drink, and said, "Maybe."

It was apparent after a few minutes more of talking to me, Bella was becoming antsy. I told her as soon as we got things situated I would get her some food, real food, and then I encouraged her to go on upstairs to check on the baby.

I hadn't eaten yet, and those two drinks went to my head. I felt a little woozy so I grabbed a small bag of chips and began to eat them on my way into the other room.

Lev looked a little better. Maybe it was my imagination, or perhaps it was the energy of the children helping him to heal.

I walked over to his makeshift bed. "Do you need me to move them away so you can get some rest?" I asked.

"No. Let them stay. I'll let you know when I need rest. We're having fun. They are taking my mind off of the pain. We are bonding."

I had news for Lev. For the rest of their lives those children would remember being in that storage crawlspace, looking up to the big man who put his life on the line for theirs.

I turned my attention toward Corbin, who seemed focused on organizing the supplies in the back of the room behind the pool table.

"Hey," I said.

"Hey." He paused and dusted off his hands. "I got all the stuff from the truck unloaded."

"I see that."

"I didn't unload the station wagon. I didn't know how long we'd be here. I put it in the back of the parking lot. You know where the woods start and the high weeds are? I've kind of stuck it in there, parked it sideways, and I leaned an old truck cab against it. Looks like an abandoned vehicle. No one will bother it."

"Thank you."

"I also brought some lanterns out. It's a lot brighter now than when I first closed the doors." He paused and exhaled heavily. "I'm afraid to ask. I ain't never seen so much blood in all my life. Even with the infected. I never seen that. It's not like I would've seen that working at the department store. She was pale. So white from all that blood loss. It was sickening. Sad, I mean, that's a better word."

"It is sad. She passed away," I said. "Ben took the baby. He's still alive. At least for now, and we're hopeful."

Almost with excitement or nervousness, Corbin nodded. "He took the baby after she died?"

"Yes."

"That sounds so much like Ben. Like something he would do."

"Yeah. In fact, he said something to that effect. Which leads me to ask you, how are you able to walk among them without being spotted and without them attacking you?"

Corbin stared at me for a second. "Don't hate me and don't judge me."

"I promise I won't."

"I got bit by my father right before we got on the boat," Corbin said. "And you know it hit me right away. I started getting sick. I was fevered and those black lines were going through me. I picked up the gun and put it to my head. Ben wouldn't let me do it. He said he would not let me turn, but he wasn't giving up. He cut away the mark on my leg. The bite wasn't real deep and then we just waited. I thought I was going to die. So many days I begged him, 'give me the gun, give me the gun'. He kept saying no. Then as fast as it hit, I woke up the next day and the fever broke. Ever since then those things don't see me. Except the dead, they do. The infected, the real dangerous ones, I can walk among them and kill them. Don't need a gun, I only need to get up close. Ben says I'm special, that I could be the cure. I don't know if I believe that, but I'm willing to try, to let them experiment on me if need be."

That explained why Ben was so adamant about wanting to get to Canada, why that was his focus. After hearing Corbin's story of survival, a bit of me wanted to go there as well.

TWENTY-THREE

PAUSE

I didn't have much interaction with the man named Philip Fleck. However, Corbin did. After Fleck came down with the baby, he and Corbin went out to get supplies. They aimed for the Rite Aid drugstore about seven miles south. When they got back, they started digging a grave for Christina.

There was a new sense of safety going out with Corbin, or sending him out, that I did not have before. When they returned they came back with boatloads of baby supplies. I prayed that it wouldn't be for naught, hoping the baby would survive to use every single ounce of formula, every diaper, and wear out every nipple on those bottles.

He was a cute little guy without a name. Ben had been favoring him, cradling him and not wanting to let go of him. I wondered if there was a sense of rebirth of his son. That if he could save one person's son, in a sense he would make up for not being able to save his own.

That was just a guess.

Corbin had gotten the story from Fleck, however, I wanted to hear it. When I asked Corbin about it, he said to ask Fleck

They hadn't eaten a real meal in over a day. Not because the Windhaven didn't have food, but because they were concerned for Christina. They didn't leave her side.

When we were reeling from our attack they were hiding in the Windhaven.

"There were twelve of us," Fleck said. "I met Christina and Bella in Georgia. The rest we met on the way. We were doing good. We'd stop, then move again, always trying to move. Movement is life."

"Ha!" I snapped, pointed at him, then pointed at Lev.

"When there were too many of those things around, we'd hunker down and wait for it to clear," Fleck went on. "It always did. They'd drop off. Recently, they've been lasting longer. We didn't move fast because Christina was pregnant. We didn't need to, so we took our time. We had enough supplies and gathered as we went. We had a pretty easy go of it. We had a goal. Until yesterday. Imagine not seeing many people, but when you did, they were all out to help each other. Everyone headed the same way, but at a different pace. Then yesterday morning just before dawn, seven men hit us. They had a load of infected in the back of a trailer. They unleashed a bunch on us when we wouldn't give them our stuff. That was after they shot four of our guys and two of our women. The other three were hit by the infected. They took everything we had. They threw Christina and she fell on her stomach. While the infected were busy..." he cringed, "we moved on foot. I knew it was too much for Christina. She was saying it wasn't, but I could see it on her face. That's when we ended up here."

They were attacked by seven men. It had to be Helena's men. Before dawn they hit Fleck's group and not long after they hit ours. They had a busy morning.

"She kept making me feel," Bella said. "Hand on her belly, check for the baby. She knew she got hurt when she fell."

"She was good most of the night," Fleck said. "Then the pain hit and the bleeding started this morning. The infected had followed us and were outside, not that we'd go anyhow. Then you guys showed. You were a godsend."

"I don't know how much of a godsend we are," I said. "Where were you headed?"

"Like everyone else," Fleck replied, "to Canada."

144

"Why does everyone want to go there?" I asked. "It can't possibly be spared."

"Listen, I know what I heard, I know that I talked to people there. So did others we've met along the way. Canada kept the infection down and it burned out. It's a safe zone."

It was different when it was just Ben and Corbin saying it. Helena insisted it was a rumor, but Fleck talked about others headed that way and how people had made radio contact.

Maybe it was a possible destination after all. I hated the thought of going into unknown territory. However, if it was a possibility, we owed it to ourselves to find out.

After Lev healed, was strong again and without a doubt, after we got our stuff back.

It was by far the best one on one time I had with my daughter in a while. Things had been so busy, sadly, I hadn't done much more than I needed to. I was sucking as a mother. She had lost her grandmother, a woman that took her under her wing, cooked for her, and taught her.

I didn't even ask Katie how she was doing with it.

Although Katie was my strong daughter, the least sensitive, she had a distorted view of the world and drew demented things that showed it. At four years old she had hardly showed that she was traumatized by what happened to the world.

The kids shared the full size bed in the other bedroom of the upstairs apartment. They lay across the width of the bed to give themselves more room.

Sawyer actually fell asleep in the bar and Corbin carried him up. I told Katie and Billy a story, even though Billy was probably thinking he was too old for it. He fell asleep, leaving me and Katie to whisper our conversation.

I kissed her goodnight, but there was a sense of anger. Yes, we were safe, but we should have been in our own cabin, our own beds.

"I'm sorry we're here," I said.

"It's okay, Mommy. At least we're together."

"That we are."

"Do you think we'll ever go home? I want to go home."

"To the cabin?" I asked. "Yes, I do."

"No. Home. Our house. I left Angeline there and a couple of ponies."

Angeline was her puppet. We had left so quickly my daughter only got to take the toys she could carry in her arms. Children need fun things, toys, and the ones she brought were probably wearing thin on her.

"Will we?" she asked.

"I don't know, but never say never." I leaned down and kissed her, said goodnight, waited for her to close her eyes, and then I left.

As I hit the bottom floor, I could hear the baby crying. Tiny shallow cries that reminded me of Addy when she was born. She didn't cry much and that worried the doctors. She only made peeping sounds and they said it was because she wasn't using her lungs.

We had to encourage her to cry. In other words, give her a reason to wail.

There was only one lantern lit and that was in the other room near Lev. The bar portion was dark, but not too dark I couldn't see to pour a drink.

Corbin was walking with the baby in his arms. He held a bottle near his mouth, but wasn't feeding him.

146

"You know, he would stop crying if you fed him."

"Not yet. He needs to open up his lungs. Hear that wimpy cry? I'll let him go another minute."

That made me smile. I had just been thinking that.

"Did you want to hold him?" Corbin asked.

"Um, no, but thanks."

"You don't like him?"

"I'm nervous around babies. Always have been. Maybe later when you need a break and after I finish my drink." I walked over to Lev and pulled up a chair. He was propped at an angle. "Does Ben know you are bent up?"

"He was the one who did it. I'm allowed to try and move tomorrow. He said the next few days he'll get me an air cast."

"Then we get a mobile Lev."

"So why are you not liking the baby?" Lev asked.

"What?" I asked innocently.

"Nila, I know you. What's up?"

"I like him. I mean, how can you not, right?" I shrugged. "I feel bad because his mother didn't want him born. She didn't want him growing up without her watching over him. As a mother, that's a horrible feeling. What if I die, who will watch Katie?"

"So if you find yourself dying you want to go ahead and take out Katie as well?"

"No! Oh my god."

"That's what you're saying."

"No, it's not, it's what Christina said and...I can understand that."

He reached out and laid his hand on mine. "We will honor his mother and protect him. What is that saying? It takes a village to raise a child, right? Well, he arrived at the village, he has a home wherever we go."

"Speaking of homes..."

"I heard you talk about going back to get our stuff at the cabin," Lev said. "You know that won't happen."

"It will."

"No, Nila, it won't. That's the past."

"Well, I have a feeling. Anyhow, Katie was talking about how she left things at the house when we left. I was thinking, when Corbin heads towards Cranberry for the air cast, maybe he and I could go to my house."

"The highway is closed."

"There are other ways I'm sure aren't blocked off."

Lev rested his head back. "Nila, is it that important? It's so dangerous."

"It is important. I never really got to say goodbye to that part of my life, to my father's house. That was our street, Lev. As you know, I don't need your permission, but I'd like to have your blessing."

"I would feel better if I was going."

"I know you would. You being in dangerous situations can't happen for a while." I rested my other hand over his. "We also don't know how long we are gonna be right here, this close. I'll be protected." I nodded my head toward Corbin. "He's a force to be reckoned with."

"How about that? Ben thinks he has immunity factors that can be useful to someone working on the virus."

"Do you honestly think there's anyone working on it? Eventually these things die. So eventually the virus will die out on its own."

"It's a vicious cycle," he said. "It won't be like the movies where people are overrun, but as long as there is one infected, there's a chance another can get it. Do I think someone's working on it?" He shook his head. "No. I also don't think there's an unscathed world in Canada."

"Everyone seems to think we're gonna cross the border and miraculously there is going to be a populated civilized world just waiting on us. It's gonna be empty."

"And cold."

"Yeah. How are we supposed to survive? We have supplies, though not nearly enough."

"If we get there and it isn't the Promised Land," Lev said, "then you, me, and Katie will head south and keep going south."

"We should just go back to the cabin," I murmured.

"I heard that." Lev squeezed my hand. "That's not going to happen and you need to accept that. Plus, isn't this what you wanted to do in the first place? Search for life?"

"Yes, but I wanted to do it on my own terms."

"Then make it your terms. We had it pretty easy, now we don't. We will again. One thing is for certain. You, me, Katie…we'll do it together."

"Trust me when I tell you, I am so grateful for that and that you are here." I leaned down and placed my lips to his hand, then to his forehead. "I missed a lot of years with you. Know this, Lev; there is nothing I wouldn't do for you now! Nothing."

Lev smiled gently. "Same."

I meant my words to my friend. I stayed with him sounding like a stuck record, repeating my worries about Canada, anger over losing the cabin, and Lev listened, until he was too tired to keep his eyes open. I had to keep reminding myself that not long before he was fighting for his life and though he acted the same, he was still healing.

After I thought to finally relieve Corbin, Ben had taken baby duty, so I decided to try to sleep.

149

I squeezed into the bed with the kids, curling up with Katie.

Despite being tired, it was hard to sleep. It wasn't my bed. I had to keep reminding myself it wasn't where I wanted to be, but at least I was with my daughter and she was safe and tight within my arms. That alone was the most important thing.

TWENTY-FOUR

MAKE A LEFT

August 16

"I think I have one," Corbin said.

"Nah, that's not it. Not big enough," replied Fleck.

I moved slowly and cautiously toward where I could hear their voices.

The two of them seemed so completely focused on finding an air cast for Lev that they were completely immune to their surroundings. That told me it wasn't new to them. I, however, was still in a state of shock because the emergency room was a totally different view of the damage done by the virus.

We had been cooped up in the Windhaven for five days. While we did go outside, we didn't wander farther than the parking lot. It felt good to get out and get moving. We monitored the radio and there was no chatter coming from Helena's camp, nor did they show up. That gave Fleck and Corbin confidence that they thought they'd gotten all they could from us and weren't coming back for more.

It was time to look for the air cast. Lev was getting antsy and though he felt better, his mobility was hindered by the plaster cast. Little did he know he wasn't going to be free of that chain quite so fast. Ben wanted us to find a cast shoe and an air cast. The cast shoe would help Lev in moving around, but in what I was certain would be to

Lev's dismay, that plaster cast wasn't coming off for several weeks. They just hadn't told him yet.

There were three types of places where the shoe and air cast could be found. A physiotherapy clinic, orthopedic surgeon's office, or emergency room.

We figured it was a case of whatever we saw first. We took all the back roads until we got to a place where the roadblocks weren't that bad and we could maneuver our way on the highway. Though we could get on to the highway, traveling on it was a bust.

Interstate 79 was a mess, four lanes of traffic all going the same way. A parking lot of cars. Some empty, some with bodies. Everyone had been fleeing the city.

There was carnage on the road, but it had been there so long it was decomposed to the point it was barely recognizable as body parts.

It was quiet. Not a bird, animal, person... nothing.

There were tons of cars, but not enough bodies. Where did they go? That many people, and/or that many infected had to be somewhere. Then again, it had been months. Cities fell first, then rural areas.

Retreating off the highway and back to the side streets led us to a hospital. I was certain we'd probably passed an orthopedic surgeon's office, but we didn't recognize it. A hospital, there was no mistaking what that was.

Outside, traffic lined the streets, cars jam packed up the driveway nearly to the door. There were decomposed bodies everywhere; the summer heat and animals had taken their toll on them. Thankfully, the virus died when the body did or else the animals would have been the next deadly wave of infection, since we knew they weren't immune.

The glass doors were busted, furniture and papers strewn out to the sidewalk. Stepping inside the emergency room entrance, I had to step over remains. There were so many decomposed body parts. The infected came in and then they turned.

Although one infected could do damage, what I witnessed was the work of many.

It didn't seem to bother Fleck or Corbin. Both of them had travelled around enough to see many places like the hospital.

"Hell, we pulled into one place," Fleck said. "Totally overrun by infected. They were having lunch."

"Yeah, us too," said Corbin.

"Guys," I winced.

"What?" Corbin asked. "You act like you've never seen any of this."

"I haven't. I left before it got like this. Closest thing I saw was Evans City and that town cleared out. So no, all these bodies? This is new for me."

Fleck patted me on the back like I was a champ. "Good job. You're handling it well."

I nodded, but inside I was thinking that I wasn't at all. I wanted to get what we needed and leave.

We did eventually find what we were looking for, along with bags of saline—a request from Ben. There was some serious discussion whether or not the air cast would fit Lev. Fleck said it fit him so it had to fit Lev.

Lev was a bigger guy. I didn't have the heart to deflate Fleck after hearing how he was a champion in the Florida independent wrestling circuit. I was just getting to know him. He too had recently been through a rough time and the three of us were actually building camaraderie on this trip.

We left the Windhaven in the morning and by early afternoon we arrived on Savannah Avenue, my street, where I not only lived with my husband and children, but where Lev and I grew up.

A cobblestone, tree lined street with Colonial brick houses so close together you could see what your neighbor was eating for dinner.

The road was more chaotic than when I had left. The street was nearly impassible with the bodies of the dead. We parked at the corner not far from my father's home and I stepped out of the truck.

Minutes before we left, insanity hit my street when a car crashed and the driver emerged infected. He began biting people, attacking. That car was still there, smashed, the driver's door still open.

There were only a few cars remaining on the street. Our neighbors must have attempted to flee. Some homes were ransacked, doors open, windows busted, furniture and supplies trailing out. Other homes were boarded up in an attempt to hold ground. I wondered what happened to them. Were they still there? Watching us?

There wasn't a sound, or any movement. Fleck and I were armed and ready just in case.

I showed them the Boswick home.

"I thought Lev lived at Big Bear?" Corbin said.

"Big Bear is a campsite," I said. "Lev and his father spent an enormous amount of time there, but like with my family, Savannah Avenue was home."

Lev's family home was one of the homes ransacked. A huge red spray painted circle with an X with writing in the middle was on the brick wall next to the door.

"The military came through," Fleck pointed out. "They searched this area. Looks like all the houses. I was in the Guard, we did this after the San Francisco quake."

"What does all that mean?" I asked.

"Top of the X is the date," Fleck said. "They came through here on June seven. The left is the unit that came though, right...it says clear, meaning nothing is in there, and the bottom zero dash zero, no survivors no bodies."

"So the INF on the Reynolds' home?" I pointed next door.

"My guess," Fleck said. "Three INF, and Zero mean three infected no bodies."

"Wow. Talk about a reality check." I pivoted to look at my father's house, and that's when I noticed it was different. The front door was open but the windows weren't busted or boarded.

"What is it?" Corbin asked.

"My father's house. Look at the markings," I said.

Just like the Boswick home, my father's house had the red circle and X, but unlike the Boswick home, above the red date of June seventh, was a date in blue, July fifteen. Additionally, in blue, 'Bio' was added to the right of the X and at the bottom was One INF.

"Someone else passed though," Fleck said. "On a later date. B."

"Bobby," I whispered and raced to the house. That date was the day Bobby arrived at the camp. Clearly he had stopped at our house, knew he was sick, and marked it down. So why did he go to the camp?

I banged my rifle against the door to make noise in case there were any infected inside. After a minute, I took a step in.

A growl and snarl preceded an infected that lunged at me.

I was ready and I fired off a shot. It sent the infected flying back into the wall. Like a cat, he bounced back, rolled, and stood.

I shot him again, only this time, he stayed down.

My father's house had been spared the ransacking, although it hadn't been immune to looters. Every cabinet was open. Lisa's chair was reclined and blood stained the arm.

I took a moment to walk around, look, take it in. That's when I realized a house doesn't make a home, the people inside do. My father, Lisa, and Bobby were gone. It was now just a dwelling.

Corbin and Fleck remained silent while inside until I walked out the door.

"Whoa, wait," Corbin called. "I think that might be for you."

How did I miss it? Maybe I didn't want to see it because of the bloody fingerprints, but a folded piece of paper was duct taped to the mantel behind the television.

"Can you grab it?" I asked. "Please. See who wrote it."

Corbin gently took it down and unfolded it. "Bobby."

My heart sank. I wanted to cry. I believed I didn't have closure with my brother, no goodbye, no last words. I was wrong.

I gratefully took the letter and held it for a moment. I would read it when we got back in the truck, after we went to my house.

I needed to absorb what it said and not while we were standing in a warzone.

I took nothing from my father's home other than that note. We left the house, closed the door, and headed down the street to my house.

It was one of the most painful experiences of my life and I would never have expected it to be. Walking into my house killed me. I was on a collision course with every memory, good and bad. Every Christmas, family dinner, were all right there. Everything we were as a family was preserved in that house. I expected to feel the way I did when I stepped into my father's house. That was not the case. Paul's blood stained the carpet by the door, there were toys on the carpet, school pictures and awards I didn't take in my rush to leave.

As strong as I wanted to be, I broke down and cried when I stepped into Addy's room. It was all her and I swore I could still smell her. I missed my daughter terribly, and though I had started moving on a bit, going home sent me right back.

It put things in perspective. I was far from healing, not even a little bit. I only hid it under the guise of being brave. I wasn't.

I stayed in my home for a while, doing nothing, saying nothing, just looking until I gathered the strength to get the items I wanted, and then we left.

We headed back to the Windhaven.

My brother's letter was brief and not as long as I'd hoped it would be.

I hope you all are good. I know you went to the cabin, but when I lost contact, I thought I would stop at the house. Maybe you came back.

I almost made it. I was attacked off of East Street just two blocks from home. Maybe I should have gone to the cabin.

I am going to try to get there. I don't know if I will make it. I shouldn't try, I just need to see you one more time.

If I don't, please know I tried, and that I love you all very much. Bobby.

Did he know then he would eventually turn? When he penned the note did he have regrets? For as intelligent as Bobby was, did he think he was immune from becoming one of those things and hurting people? Maybe he just didn't know that somewhere in his infected brain a memory would lead him home.

I know everyone thinks I'm nuts for believing that, but I knew it was true.

My feelings were all over the place. I was a mess. Sad. Angry. I felt bad for not being there for my brother, guilty that our last exchange was a bloody note he wrote while facing death alone.

After reading that letter six times, I folded it and placed it inside the high school yearbook I brought from my house.

We were close to the cabin turnoff. The exit sign for Big Bear was actually a double entendre to me.

"Stop," I said softly to Corbin.

He did. "What's wrong?"

"Can you turn?"

"Right here?"

I nodded.

"Nila, that's...that road..."

"I know where it goes. We'll be careful, but there's something...there's something I need to see."

Corbin stared at me for a second, looking into my eyes as if he sensed what I needed. Without questioning any further, he made the turn.

TWENTY-FIVE

FROM LEV'S SIDE

Even if I was worried, I couldn't show it. Not to Katie. Once Nila left with Corbin and Fleck she started with odd stories. At one point I hoped she wasn't getting psychic premonitions. Then again, I had to remember that Katie was a strange child.

Not as strange as Corbin, I didn't understand why he asked such odd questions. Off the wall, off topic questions in the middle of a conversation.

The Boy Scout question made sense, he was alluding to the smoke signals. Some of the other ones were completely off the wall.

As they prepared to leave, he asked Nila, "You aren't planning on picking flowers again, are you?"

Ben scratched his head on that one, but was still confident in it having a meaning.

"I can assure you, every question he asks means something," Ben said. "Since his infection he doesn't process thoughts normally. Yeah, some of his questions are facetious, but most he gets these images in his mind, thoughts, and can't organize them, so he asks an off the wall question to try to trigger the memory or thought."

It didn't quite make sense to me. Ben explained further using the 'did we like cats' question when we first met him. Ben was certain that it had to do with the infected cats we saw, but Corbin couldn't process that it was what he wanted to say.

However, Corbin had a special ability. One that couldn't be denied.

"Do you think Canada is the place to go?" I asked Ben. "You are so confident about it."

"Radio talk, people talk, even before everything fell apart it was said that Canada had shut down borders, set up quarantines."

"But no one has heard anything from the north."

"What's it going to hurt?" Ben asked.

"I just would rather be somewhere warm when winter comes."

"We have the generators, we can get gas, it's worth a shot. I really believe that."

Everyone believed that.

We were now nomads. We lost our home, if we had the means to survive and make the journey, then trying was the right thing to do.

I promised myself right then and there not to second guess the journey north. If it was a dead end, it wasn't like we were trapped. We could turn around.

They were gone a while. With each passing hour, I worried more, and Katie didn't help. I found it much more comfortable to sit with half my rear on a barstool than lying down all the time.

Katie followed me everywhere making sure I didn't fall when I balanced holding on to things and didn't walk too much.

"Do you think she's okay?" she asked.

"I do. Corbin is a good source of protection."

"Because he got bit like me?"

"Yes, somewhat."

"Do you think I have special abilities like Corbin?"

I shrugged. "I don't know. Let's not test that." I winked. "Corbin actually had the infection."

"What if he still does?" she asked.

"He doesn't."

"What if he does and at any second he could turn?"

I was ready to dismiss that, and started to laugh, then I thought about what she said. As a precaution, I asked Ben. He actually did laugh.

I had estimated how long it would take them to go around and get to Edgewood, added some time for stops. I figured six hours was plenty, seven was pushing it. When it neared the ten hour mark, I was getting panicky. Then Sawyer spotted them from upstairs.

"They're coming down the road. They have stuff!" Sawyer said excitedly from upstairs.

I carefully inched my way to the door, ready to open it and even yell at them for taking so long.

"Cool!" Sawyer shouted. "Fleck's riding a motorcycle!"

I opened the door as they pulled close.

"Hey, big guy." Corbin stepped from the truck. "We got your booties."

"Now you can be mobile," Nila said.

"You guys were gone a while. Everything okay?"

Nila looked at Corbin before answering. "Yeah."

Then I saw the gas cans. "Where did they come from?" I asked.

"Oh, you know," Nila said nonchalantly. "It's the apocalypse, we found them."

"And the motorcycle?" I asked, my eyes focused on the bike.

"Yeah, hey…" Nila nudged me. "Look what I…Lev, what's wrong?"

"You got all this stuff out there?"

"Why are you so suspicious? We're leaving for Canada. We need it for the trip. I got our yearbook. You need to see it."

I don't know why, but something didn't feel right, and as soon as I got a good look at the bike I knew what it was.

"Nila, is that my bike?"

"What?"

"It was up at Big Bear. Is that my bike?"

"Lev…"

Hand against the truck for support, I moved slowly to the bike. Nila followed me, almost as if trying to stop me. As soon as I saw the plate, I knew it was. I spun around. "Forty people took over that camp. Some really dangerous people. How did you get the bike back?"

"We took it," she said.

"We did," Corbin stated. "We snuck in there and grabbed it. Along with a few other things."

My eyes widened. "Nila, we have kids here. Do you know what kind of risk this is?"

She shook her head. "It's not a risk."

"Yes, it is. They're going to come looking for us when they know you raided the camp."

"No, Lev, they won't." Nila turned serious and turned and walked away from me. At the same time, there was a weird, awkward silence. Corbin and Fleck instantly occupied themselves.

I reached out and took hold of her arm.

"What?" Nila snapped.

I looked down at her, examining her eyes. For the first time that I could recall, I saw a coldness there. "Nila," my voice cracked. "what did you do?"

TWENTY-SIX

THE MUSIC

August 17

In my entire life I was never able to lie to Lev. I couldn't look him in the eye and lie. Except at the end of our friendship, when I told him I never wanted anything to do with him again. That was the first and last time I was angry with Lev until now.

Lev was an honest man, a good soul, and he had a righteous side that came out after we returned. He insisted on knowing how we got the gas and the motorcycle. He assumed the worst of us. I didn't want to tell him he was right.

I did tell him it was too late to deal with it and I was tired and wanted to just hang out with Katie. The next day I would tell him everything.

Bella was on baby duty and woke Ben to tell him that Christian, the name he had given to the baby, was warm and his nose was stuffy.

Ben didn't think the baby had anything life threatening, but he determined that the child was too young to go anywhere yet and it was putting him at risk.

The plan of packing everything we could, including supplies from the Windhaven, was out the window.

Fleck mentioned that he and his group always moved at their own pace and he wanted us to still go, saying he would stay behind with the baby. Bella wasn't leaving Fleck, but more surprising was Ben. He wasn't going to leave the baby.

"You can go. Leave word, leave signs," Ben said. "We'll find you. We're not going to leave for a couple of weeks so if you don't come back, we'll know you made it."

Going to Canada was all Ben's idea and now he wasn't going to go? It was approaching fall, and if Canada was actually an option we needed to know. If it wasn't, we had to hunker down for the cold months.

"We'll all wait," Lev said. "We'll all go together."

"No, we need to know if Canada is a go," Ben insisted. "We need to get Corbin there. If they're infection free, they won't be for long."

"What about sending Corbin first, maybe do the search party?" I suggested. "Like we originally planned."

"And wait out here?" Ben asked.

"No," I replied. "We wait at the cabin."

Lev spun his body toward me. "Your father's cabin?"

I nodded.

"That's not an option."

"It is now. It needs cleaned," I said, "but it's an option. Ben, Fleck, Bella, and the baby can hole up there. Or we all can while we do a scouting party. Either way, it's out of the way and..." Lev limped to the door, moving slowly and awkwardly in the cast shoe and holding his side. "Where are you going?"

He paused before walking out. "To the cabin."

Lev was in no physical condition to travel to the cabin, especially alone. So Corbin and I went with him.

<><><><>

165

I couldn't figure out Lev's mood, why he seemed so angry. I attributed it to the fact that he just didn't feel well. He was a man who was used to doing, always going. Yet he was bound by the limitations of his body and they were out of his control.

"You were in no condition to leave," I told him in the truck as we headed to my father's cabin.

"I was fine enough to make the trip to Canada," he argued.

"That's different."

"How?"

"Because that would only require you to ride. You want to get out and walk around," I said.

"No, I want to see why it's fine all of a sudden to return to your father's cabin. A week ago we were hiding and on the run."

"Things change."

"Like what?"

I didn't respond.

We pulled as close to the fence of my father's property as we could so Lev wouldn't have to walk far. He stood at the gate staring in at the body riddled yard of my father's land.

A few tents had been erected, they appeared to have toppled. It was evident that a lot of chaos that occurred. The land was a mess.

Even dead, it was clear they were infected when they died.

Corbin stepped forward. "I went on the property and took them out today," he said. "They were infected. Freshly turned and in that highest energy stage."

"How many?" Lev asked.

166

"Ten," I said. "I haven't been in the cabin. Corbin said they had come out. No one's inside. Only this outer area needs cleaned. We can get it cleaned and have a safe place to stay."

"How?" Lev asked. "Any ideas how all these people got infected?"

Corbin glanced at me. "Nila's theory is right. There's something in them that moves them on memory. We found Lester shot up just outside the fence."

"How did Lester get out?" Lev asked. "Do you think they freed him?"

I looked at Corbin.

"I took Lester out and released him at Big Bear," Corbin admitted. "I figured he could wreak a little havoc. He came back here somehow. That memory thing I guess. I don't know." Corbin scratched his head. "He could have attacked this camp too. It's hard to tell. But the infected are here. More than likely they put them here to turn, run their course, and die. We all know how fast this virus spreads."

"When we got here they were running around the property and couldn't get out," I said.

"So the cabin and the land is secure and safe?" Lev asked, and Corbin nodded. "Here's what I don't get, if they knew they were infected, why didn't they just kill them?"

Corbin shrugged. "That's a mystery."

"Here's another," Lev said. "What made you come back here? We left a week ago, what made you come back?"

"Simple," Corbin answered. "I released Lester. I wanted to see if he caused damage. He did. Threat's over. It's finished. We can move back."

"What about the other forty or so people?" Lev asked.

167

Without hesitation Corbin replied, "It was a bluff. We think that woman in the blue is Helena. For sure Scott is in this group."

"A bluff, huh?" Lev asked. "You said you think they moved the infected here. Who would move them if it was a bluff?"

"I said that?" Corbin asked. "Wow. Slip of the tongue."

"So you went to Big Bear?" Lev asked.

"Why are you so suspicious?" I questioned.

"Because it's not this easy," Lev said. "We got shot up and you two defeated them all with one infected? It doesn't make sense."

"What does it matter?" I asked. "We have our place back."

"It matters, Nila. We got our place back at what cost?"

"At what cost did they take it?"

Lev nodded once. "Let's take a ride to Big Bear."

"No," I said adamantly. "Let it go and let's get this place cleaned up."

"Why? Is it because they really are there?" Lev asked. "If they are, that's too close for us to move back here. That's asking for a repeat."

"It won't happen," I said.

"How do you know?"

"Because," I said. "They're all dead."

"They're *all* dead?" Lev asked.

"Yes."

"How?"

Before I could reply, Corbin answered, "They're dead because I killed them. Let's leave it at that."

The explanation wasn't enough for Lev, although I didn't understand why. It was no surprise that we headed to Big Bear.

All the way there, I kept wondering why it was important to him. Why did he need to investigate our claim like a bad detective? The bottom line was we had our property back, end of story. Not to Lev. For some reason it mattered.

We really tried to convince Lev he didn't need to see Big Bear. The more we connived, the more he insisted.

We pulled into Big Bear, stopping just inside the main gate. There were new vehicles everywhere, not a person in sight.

Stepping from the truck, the smell of bodies was overwhelming, yet there wasn't a body to be seen. Lev didn't need to see a body to know it was a dead camp.

Even though he was moving slowly, Lev looked around. He didn't need to search far. The first camper gave him the answer.

Two men and one woman were inside. In a sickly state, they had crawled into a bed. Their ravaged bodies were in a state of decay, but remnants of a violent death were evident.

Not a bloody violent death. An illness. Dried vomit and fecal matter encircled their bodies, creating even more of a horrendous smell. Pails, buckets, and towels were beside the bed. They were weak, vomiting, had diarrhea, and didn't have the strength to move from the bed.

It was obvious they weren't infected and by the rate of their decomposition, they were dead longer than the people at my father's cabin.

I saw the horror on Lev's face. He was in that first camper for only a moment when he left.

"Is it everywhere at Big Bear?" he asked.

"Yes," I answered.

"Do you think it was a new form of the virus? Maybe it mutated in a different way."

Right then and there I had a choice. I could just go along with the new virus theory or tell the truth.

I never could lie to Lev.

"It wasn't a virus," I said. "It was poison."

Lev had an odd, slow motion reaction. He slowly turned his head toward me, his brown eyes piercing my way. "They were poisoned?"

I nodded.

"You poisoned the well." It was a statement not a question.

"I did," Corbin interjected. "She didn't. Lester was a diversion. They didn't see it coming."

"Oh, yeah?" Lev raised his eyebrows. "How?"

"How what?"

"How did you poison them?"

"A little of this, a little of that."

Lev shifted his eyes to me then back to Corbin as he nodded. "As valiant as it is to take responsibility for her actions, Nila knows poison. She knows every root, seedling, berry, and plant around this area, what is poisonous and what isn't. Don't you?"

"Yeah, I do."

"How do you know it was a plant?" Corbin asked. "It could be rat poisoning, or a whole bunch of other stuff."

Lev kept his eyes on me. "Because rat poison would be strong to the taste."

"If they don't know well water," Corbin said, "they wouldn't know it wasn't supposed to taste like that. So you can't say it was her. They killed *my* mother, Lev. I wanted them dead. What difference does it make who did it? It's done."

"Because I need to know if the woman I have known most of my life is capable of something like poisoning the well."

170

"Technically," I said, "it was the pressure tank."

"Nila!" he snapped. "It's the same difference."

"No, Lev it isn't! You know that. If I poisoned the well everything would be toxic. I just shut down the intake, knowing by the time they noticed it wasn't pumping it would be too late."

"Oh my God," Lev said in shock.

Both my father's land and Big Bear operated on well water. We had one automatic pump and the rest were hand pumps. We had to fill the reserve tanks by hand. There was no running water unless pumped directly. Big Bear was different. They had running water and showers. In order for that to happen, the well water pumped into a pressure tank. I was quite sure that those who took over the campsite didn't have a clue. In fact, I was banking on it.

"How?" Lev asked.

"Nature provides," I said. "I took advantage of it. Like Corbin said, a little of this, a little of that…"

"You had no clue it would work."

"None. Still, I had to try, and I don't understand why you are acting like this."

"Did you expect me to be happy?"

"No, but I didn't expect you to be so righteous about it. Maybe even be a little grateful."

"Grateful!" Lev sputtered.

At that point, Corbin backed up.

"Nila you killed—no, wait, you *murdered* forty people. You pulled a Jim Jones on them."

I don't know why, but Lev's attempt at being serious and referencing the Jonestown kool aid massacre made me laugh.

"You think this is funny?" he asked.

"No, I don't. What was I supposed to do? Just say 'Here, take the land, enjoy, have a great life' and go away quietly?"

"Yes."

"No! They came and took what they wanted. They took my land, your land, places our fathers built with their own hands. They killed our people, shot you, raided us like we were nothing. I wasn't sitting by and letting it go."

"It was murder!"

"It was justice!" I shrieked. "There are no laws, no cops for me to run to. I had a choice and I made it. Was it vengeful? Yes. It's a land without law and order. It was also an eye for an eye, plain and simple, frontier justice."

"Who appointed you judge, jury, and executioner?"

"I did."

"You had no right."

"I had every right. Fuck you for your holier than thou attitude and passing judgment on me. What I did is my burden, I have to live with it, not you."

"I have to live with you," he said.

"Well then don't."

Lev gasped and stepped back. "I don't know what bothers me more. The fact that you killed all these people, or the fact that it doesn't even bother you."

He turned and headed back toward the truck.

Corbin walked up to me. "You okay?"

"Yeah." I exhaled and looked at him. "It does bother me you know, what I did. I tried not to think about it, a part of me was hoping it didn't work."

"It did."

172

"I know."

"For what it's worth. I'm glad." He placed his hand on my back. "No matter what, this cannot be in vain. You cleared the camp, don't let it be for nothing."

Corbin was right. I got my home back and even if what I did was wrong, I had to find a way to show that in some ways it was worth it.

That was easier said than done.

TWENTY-SEVEN

RESOLVE

August 19

If it was Lev's intention to make me feel guilty, he failed. Maybe one day in the future it would hit me what I had done. Any inkling of bad I felt was gone when Corbin, Fleck, and I returned to the cabin. A place I have known and loved since childhood, a place built by my father. It was destroyed by those who invaded it.

How dare Lev Judge me? I thought. *Look at what they did!*

Even though they were infected, the rage didn't do this...spite did.

My stepmother Lisa, in an attempt to keep the kids occupied, had started a history mural. Every day she and the kids would color or paint a drawing on the long piece of drywall. It was art, a remembrance of my daughter who died. It was some of her life force.

They destroyed it. It lay crumbled, white dust spreading about the cabin, and when I saw that I desperately sought any remnants of Addy's drawings. There wasn't much.

My mother's picture was smashed. The cabin was in disarray, and the worst was our little cemetery. Those we loved and lost were not only buried there, their graves were preciously marked. Those vile bastards ran over the graves with a truck as if they were teenagers pulling a cemetery prank.

They smeared shit all over the outhouse. I knew they had no clue about the well system and I had shut it down, hoping that if the poison didn't work, the lack of water would.

They desecrated my home.

Thankfully, Lester made a comeback somehow and infected those who were there.

I didn't need justification for what I had done. All I had to do was look around. I didn't feel guilty, I felt enraged and glad every single one of them was dead.

There was no way we would get the cabin clean and ready in one day. When we returned, that first day was body clean up only. We loaded them in one of their trucks, took the bodies thirty miles east, and burned them.

That night we returned to Windhaven. Lev didn't look at me and quite frankly I didn't look at him. It was like a repeat of history between us.

For some reason—I wrongly, I found out—I lumped Ben into that judgmental group with Lev. When he approached me about what occurred, I handed him attitude.

"I really don't want to hear it," I said.

"Hear what? I'm just asking," Ben said. "Are they all dead?"

"Yes," I snapped.

"Okay. When can we go back to the cabin?"

I exhaled. "Two days. We'll get it clean, get you situated, then we'll prepare to go to Canada."

"It will be a lot easier getting ready when we're at the cabin."

"Yeah, it will be. Your RV is...let's say it needs to be cleaned."

"Edi's pop up trailer?" Ben asked.

"No. Someone spent their last hours in there before they turned and you know how bloody that can be. We're gonna pull it from the property."

"Do you need my help?"

"No we got this." I squeezed his arm. "Thank you for not judging me."

I started to walk away.

"Nila, listen…" Ben inched toward me. "It's a shock thing, you know. It's not judgment."

I huffed out a laugh. "Ben, you didn't hear him."

"Yeah, I did. I heard what he told me. Then I heard what he told Katie and the boys."

"Which was?"

"He said that you took care of things and everything is going to be okay. The cabin is ours again. The kids didn't ask why and he didn't elaborate, but he didn't present you as a killer."

"I should hope not, my daughter is four."

"I'm just saying, he knows. Give him time."

Lev and I didn't speak to each other and the only interaction we had was when we switched baby duty. The next day, I thanked Ben for watching Katie then Corbin, Fleck, and I left for the cabin.

Getting the cabin cleaned up was easier than I expected. Corbin took the really dirty job, saying he didn't mind because he'd worked at a department store.

"Ever see a women's rest room?" he asked.

It was another exhausting day, and the next morning we began moving supplies. We took everything we could from the Windhaven. Every can of corn, roll of toilet paper, towels, and booze. If it wasn't nailed down we took it.

By that evening we had dinner…at the cabin.

Sitting around the table, we spread out a map and planned our route to Canada. Being back in the cabin surrounded by familiarity, knowing what the world was like outside our safety fence, had me doubting I wanted to leave.

After getting the kids down for the evening, I checked the shed and storage. It was packed. Since Helena's people arrived in a convoy, we had our pick of vehicles for the trip. Corbin was getting one road ready, a station wagon, and when last I checked Lev was loading supplies for the trip.

It hadn't been that long but I missed my nightly routine of sitting on the porch step. I grabbed my glass along with the bottle and walked through the cabin. Bella was on the couch holding the baby.

"You should get some sleep," she said. "You have a long trip to-morrow."

"I will. I want to wind down. It was my tradition here." I lifted the drink.

"Thank you for letting us stay here," she said. "I love it."

"You know, when I was your age, I hated it here. My father forced me to come here. The only saving grace was Lev. Now I love it."

"You don't want to go, do you?" she asked.

"Not really. We have to try though. If there is a civilized world out there, we have to find it. It's scary to think the world has ended. It's even scarier to think we may be the only country in ruins. Imagine that. How long would they let us be?"

177

Her eyes filled with horror.

"Oh, I'm sorry. I forgot you're young. Forget I said anything."

"Yeah, I don't think that's happening anytime soon," she said.

I smiled and laid my hand on her shoulder. "Let me know if you need a break."

"I will. I'm fine."

Drink in hand I headed outside to enjoy what could be my last night on the porch.

I sat there in thought, wondering what the road ahead would hold, what the days ahead would bring. If Canada was indeed a live country, then what would entering be like?

I had been there for a while having my second drink when Lev came over and without saying a word sat next to me.

After a long thirty seconds, Lev took the bottle and sipped from it while staring straight ahead. "Twenty-two years ago you gave me a long hard stare, turned away from me, and never spoke to me again," he said tonelessly. "The closest thing there was to reconnecting was when you friend requested me on social media six years ago."

I took the bottle. "I didn't do it. Bobby was in town, staying over. I was logged on and he did it. He also put a bogus post about how great a brother I had." I set down the bottle. "For what it's worth, I didn't cancel the friend request."

"Thank you for that."

"You're welcome."

"I won't have it again," Lev said. "I won't go half my life without speaking to you."

"Kind of tough if we're gonna survive this thing."

"Even then, things can be strained. I don't want that."

"Neither do I," I said. "But I'm not apologizing."

"I'm not asking to you to."

"And I won't get into a moral discussion."

"It will be a non-discussion."

"Deal."

Silence.

"I know you hate what happened," I said.

"I thought we weren't talking about this."

"I have to say one thing." I lifted a finger. "Do you think I'm proud of what I did?"

"You want me to answer that?" Lev asked.

"Yes."

"Then yes. I think you are."

"I'm not. But I'm not ashamed either. Not yet. I may be, just not yet. I did what I believed had to be done." I poured more into my glass and handed Lev the bottle.

"I understand that. Just understand that I never believed you to be capable of something like that."

"Well…" I exhaled, "I have a vengeful side."

"Since when?"

"Since eighth grade. Remember when Belinda cut the back of my hair? We all thought I was passive. I wasn't. I plotted, I planned, and I got my revenge," I said. "Eighth grade picnic. She was carrying a purse, and when you're in eighth grade and carry a purse it means one thing. You're on your period. I waited, and when she wasn't looking, I took her pads from her purse. She didn't have any feminine protection the whole picnic, bled right through her white shorts."

Lev stared at me for a moment in disbelief. "Nila, this is hardly the same thing."

"Yeah, well, you've never been a teenage girl with visible menstrual blood on the back of her pants. It's the end of the world."

"I'll take your word for it." He extended his hand. "Friends?"

"Friends." I took his hand.

Lev cupped my hand gently then surprising me, leaned over and kissed me quickly and softly on the lips before squeezing my hand. He released it and lifted the bottle to his lips. "So…" he said, "are you ready for tomorrow?"

"I have mixed emotions. Especially since we're back here."

"I hear you," Lev said. "I would like not to leave. However, I think if we don't, we'll always wonder. If there's a chance that somewhere out there's a world still in existence we need to look. I heard what you said to Bella."

"You mean about if we're the only one in ruins?"

Lev nodded. "I can't imagine what the rest of the world would want to do with us. That's why we need to know as well."

"Are you concerned about us traveling with the kids? After Fleck told us the ambush story, that scares me more than the infected."

"Me too. Last week proved we're not safe here. We may think it, feel it, but we're not a hundred percent safe. We'll never be no matter where we go," Lev said.

"Can I ask you something?"

He nodded.

"Doesn't look like you're packing much."

"I'm not. Enough to get there and back."

"So you're planning on there not being anything in Canada?"

"No," he said. "I'm planning on there being people there. Lots."

I looked at him confused. "I don't understand. Why not take a lot of stuff, especially if we're not coming back?"

"Oh, we'll be back eventually. But if you think about it, if Canada is a safe zone, they're not going to stand at the border waving their arms saying, 'hey come on in', there'll be a vetting process. They'll take our weapons and we'll have to hand over a lot of our stuff. I'd rather not have it with us."

"What makes you think that?" I asked.

"If refuges from an infected country were coming here, do you think we'd just freely let them in without checking?"

"No. So you think that's the way it is?"

"I don't know. It could be. It could also be the guy waving us in." He paused. "Or it could be like the Green Area. A short lived promising place that fell. I believe that is the most probable."

"It was fine a while back but now it's not you mean?" I asked.

"That's what I think. Then again, time will let us know."

"If all goes as planned, twenty-four hours from now, we'll know."

TWENTY-EIGHT

BEYOND BORDERS

August 21

If there was one useful thing that Helena's people brought with them, it was the radio system. We delayed our trip to Canada one more day to get the radios up and running. Open communication with Ben was best, but as a Plan B, Lev had made wooden spikes that we would use instead of breadcrumbs.

The route was pretty straightforward, all highway driving. As long as the roads were semi-passable, we were good. The shortest distance to the point of entry into our neighbor was through Buffalo. We would take a route around Erie, Pennsylvania, since we knew that was down.

Saying goodbye wasn't hard because it didn't seem like a forever goodbye. Ben had the hardest time saying goodbye to the kids. He knew if we stayed in Canada, he'd see us in a month or so when Christian was able to travel.

"Remember," Ben said to Lev, "when you get there, have them look at that leg and stomach."

"I feel confident I had the best doctor," Lev replied.

Ben was such an asset, a part of me really wished he was going with us. If there was a government running north of us, Ben would be an entry ticket.

We left behind almost everything and took only the minimum. After all, we were only traveling a short distance. Returning was an option. Our problem was not a single one of us had been north of Erie. We had no clue what was up there. All communication with other camps had come from the south or west, nothing north.

Thinking about my radio contact with them pissed me off. How much I trusted them and believed we shared a common interest.

Helena had invited us to her camp. Was that authentic? What about Hal? He genuinely seemed nice. Did Helena wipe him out too?

Who Helena was, if that was even her real name, would never be known. I saw the body of a woman I believed could have been Helena. She was in a camper not far from the main entrance. A larger woman with many lines on her face, even dead she looked rough and like I envisioned her. There were twelve women who died in Big Bear. One died at my father's cabin. Of them all, she was the most likely.

We left as soon as the sun was up, giving us the whole day for the journey. If it was a bust, we'd spend the night and return. Been there done that before.

It was a given that Buffalo, the nearest entry point, would not pan out. Erie was still blocked, and going around it wasn't much better. There was a horde of infected that moved like a wave of destruction north. Were they following life or were they, like I suspected, following memory and instinct? So many of them had backpacks.

Since it was months after the initial outbreak, I had to wonder where that many infected came from.

Around Erie and just beyond it we saw a lot of bodies. Though some were badly decomposed, most weren't even in one piece. That happened when they moved in their dead state. The decay caused them to pull apart limb by limb until nothing was left.

A little farther on they were still moving. Struggling, crawling along the ground with their lower torsos trailing behind, connected only by tendons and intestines.

The closer we got to Buffalo, the more we full blown infected we saw. The mindless migration proved that even with the infected, only the strong survived.

A part of me even wondered if father north we'd see uninfected moving.

"Why this progression?" I asked. I sat in the middle of the back seat, the kids staring out the windows on either side. Billy was trying to count the infected. "Back there were dead. Here are infected."

The highway a hundred miles before Buffalo was pretty clear, only infected moved down it. We tried not to hit them because we didn't want any damage to the wagon.

"I think people got the memo," Corbin said. "I think they were headed to Canada. Those who were infected father south died near Erie."

"They probably infected more before they dropped," Lev said. "They in turn infected people. It was a domino effect."

"Where are they all coming from? Were there that many people that survived?"

"Nila, we haven't seen much of the world. We saw a small fraction of the country. They could have come from all over," Lev said. "Look at Fleck and Bella. They traveled."

"Plus," Corbin said, "think about it. Even at a low one percent not affected out of four hundred million Americans, that's four million healthy and fine. If half of them died for unknown reasons that's still two million people heading north."

I laughed. "I doubt two million people are headed north."

"One percent of them? That's twenty-thousand refugees," Corbin said.

"That's pretty good," Lev said.

Corbin pointed to his temple. "Math whiz. Did you have a big television?"

"What?" I laughed my question.

"And there it is." Lev lifted his hand and dropped it. "You ask questions out of the blue. It's been a while so one was due."

"That wasn't out of the blue," Corbin defended.

"We're talking about percentage of population and you ask about the TV size."

"Because I learned about this on the History Channel. Geez. Hell, there's more people left now than in 1800." Corbin shook his head. "Out of the blue question. Good Lord, bet you feel dumb now."

"No," Lev said. "Not at all."

We tested the radio each time we made a stop for one of the kids to go to the bathroom. I hated stopping simply because we didn't know if any infected would race out toward us.

Just before Buffalo, it was apparent that my suspicions were correct. On a large green sign that listed Buffalo exits was a spray painted message. A large arrow blocked out the exits signs. On top of the arrow it read: **Buffalo Dead, no CA entry**, below it, **Take 20 to 1,000 Isl.**

It was easy to decipher. Avoid Buffalo, it was dead and there was no access to Canada, take alternate route.

We discussed it a little then radioed Ben. Should we keep going or turn around? That sign could have been painted months earlier. A lot could happen in a month.

It was decided we'd move forward. According to the map, Thousand Island Bridge and Border Patrol was another three hour drive. That wasn't much. If it was a bust, we'd go back to the cabin.

We didn't see any cars, no traffic at all. Not that we expected to, we also didn't see any infected after Buffalo.

Corbin joked, "Maybe the infected remembered they had to go to Canada but couldn't read."

I didn't think that was funny, as I believed it to be true.

Three bathroom stops and nearly four hours later, we hit the north stretch of highway that went from Watertown, New York to the Wesley Islands, and the Thousand Island Bridge.

We passed through Alexandria Bay and everything was so green and peaceful. The winding road gave us a view of the lakes, the air smelled fresh, and I believe we saw only one body on the side of the road.

It was exactly two miles to the border and bridge that everything came to a complete halt. All lanes across the highway were packed with cars, both sides utilized for inbound traffic across the border.

If traffic was stopped surely there were people. We didn't see a soul.

"Stay here." Corbin opened the door and stepped out.

Corbin walked ahead, looking in cars.

There was a bit of disappointment on Lev's face. I think a part of him deep inside really wanted there to be a safe zone in Canada.

"Empty!" Corbin yelled. "They're all empty." He walked a little farther, then after a football field length, returned.

"Bodies?" Lev asked.

"None," Corbin answered. "In fact, some of these cars have no dust on them. They haven't been here long."

"We gotta get out of here," I said. "This many cars means that many infected around here."

"I agree," Lev said. "Let's radio Ben and head home."

While I loved that cabin and I didn't mind going back, I truly wanted to believe a world was still in existence somewhere, that there was a fight for life instead of an easy road into extinction.

My heart sank with disappointment that I didn't want to show the kids.

We tried. We failed.

Defeated, we approached the car and that was when we heard a helicopter.

My eyes widened. Filled with excitement I spun around to Lev. "Do you hear that?"

The whirling blades grew louder and I nearly shrieked.

It was so loud the kids jumped out of the car and Corbin raced over to Sawyer, lifting him in his arms and pointing to the sky.

The chopper hovered above our heads and then a male voice came over a speaker. *"Attention refugees. Ontario and Quebec are infection free zones. Leave all belongings behind and proceed on foot."* The message was then repeated in French. *"Attention, les réfugiés. Ontario et du Québec sont des zones d'infection libre. Laissez tous les biens derrière et continuer à pied."*

The helicopter flew onward, and the same message repeated in English. It was a recording.

Corbin placed down Sawyer, grabbed the radio, and called Ben. "We made it," Corbin said. "There's life."

TWENTY-NINE

RULES

We did as instructed, but like many others we moved our wagon off to the side in case we needed to go back for it. We secured our belongings in the back under the floor hatch and buried the keys by the passenger front tire.

Kids in tow, we walked the last two miles. The helicopter circled around every ten minutes repeating the message. As we got closer to the border we could see others like us walking north. Small groups spread out, probably families like ours.

All of those rumors that had traveled by word of mouth and radio chatter were true.

I could feel civilization. We left at seven in the morning and before four in the afternoon we would be walking into a safe zone. An area of the world that didn't have the infection.

On the United States side of the border, right before the crossing, were armed Canadian soldiers standing guard.

Before going across the bridge, we could see people stopping to read a sign. When we arrived there, we did the same.

On top of the sign, bright and bold it stated:

Please Read.

You are entering an infection free zone. In order to keep our country safe, you will be asked to sign a health declaration. No one with visible signs of infection, bites, or scratches from the infected will be admitted. It is an executable crime to attempt to conceal any bites or infection and enter the country. Though severe, we ask that you understand. It is for your safety and ours. Welcome.

"What's it say, Mommy?" Katie asked.

"It says they are not going down without a fight. That they keep all sick people out."

Katie smiled at me. "We'll be safe. No more monsters."

"No more monsters." I hugged her then looked at Lev. "We made it."

He grinned. "We made it."

At the border there were more armed soldiers and each of us was stopped and visually scanned. Even though we all signed that health declaration stating we weren't sick, Lev drew suspicion. He had hit his limit of exhaustion and looked bad. The walk did him in.

"He's not infected," I said. "He was shot and his leg is fractured."

They let us through, gave us a copy of our papers, told us to go to the check in building to be assigned temporary living quarters, and the guard made a radio call as we walked to the next station.

It was a large camp that was buzzing with people and structures set up everywhere.

As we arrived at the check in building, Lev was intercepted.

"We need to take him to the medical building for evaluation," the man said. "We'll release him after everything checks out."

"I understand," I said.

I didn't mind the extra security. After all, it was for our benefit as well.

Children were running about the camp and Katie, Sawyer, and Billy were pretty excited about that.

"Will we be able to play with them, Mommy?" Katie asked.

"I'm sure, sweetie." Upon registering our group, we made our first mistake.

We didn't claim Billy as family. We told the truth that his father and mother had passed away.

"We have a wonderful orphans program," the woman told us.

"That won't be necessary," I said. "He's with us."

"I don't think you understand," she explained. "He *has* to be placed in the orphan center. We have many Americans coming across looking for family. He may have family wanting to find him. You can see him and visit him, but we need to have him in the center for thirty days. That way if we release him to you, you'll have a permanent residence and we'll have record of his location should someone come looking for him."

A thirty day lost and found for children. It reminded me of Arby's. If we found money or anything and turned it in, it was ours if unclaimed after thirty days.

As hard as it was for all of us, we didn't have a choice. We said our goodbyes to Billy and told him we'd see him in a few hours. He cried and it broke my heart. "We won't be far," I told him. "We're just in the camp."

We were each given a small box of clothing and we carried them as we were escorted to our tent.

I jumped at the sound of a gunshot.

"No worries," our soldier escort told us. "We get a lot of people sneaking in with infection. It sounds harsh, I know, but it is the only way to keep the infection away. Each month we have fewer sneaking in. In a few months no one will come in with infection."

"Why don't you kick them out?" I asked.

"And put them where? Back in the US? So they can and infect someone else?" He shook his head. "Stop it early. It's what's best for them as well. You'll see."

Corbin whispered, "Ben would totally disagree with this."

"Their home their rules, right?"

"I guess."

Corbin was leery. I would be too if I didn't see so many people and they didn't look miserable or scared. Some waved to us as we walked by. They were comfortable and relaxed, making the best of their new home in a safe zone.

As horrible as the executions sounded, I understood it. Unlike the Green Area in Ohio, there was very little chance of the camp being overrun.

Our escort showed us to our tent. Since there were five of us, we had our own. Six cots were in the tent, along with a table. We were given a box of Meals Ready to Eat and were sorting through them and our new clothes when the flap to the tent opened in a rush.

Lev stepped in. His eyes were saddened and he said hurriedly, "Nila, I'm sorry. I'm so sorry."

Instantly, I panicked. Was he infected and we didn't know? What was going on?"

A man in a mask entered, along with an armed soldier who wouldn't look at us.

"Lev? What's going on?" I asked.

"They asked who fixed me," Lev said. "I told them about Ben and how he's the reason we're here. I made the mistake of telling them that Corbin was a cure and—"

The man in the mask stepped up to Corbin. "Were you bitten?"

Corbin was pretty nonchalant about it. "Yeah, but no big deal. It was months ago. I never got sick. See?" He rolled up his tee shirt sleeve to expose the healed bite mark and surgery site.

The soldier aimed at Corbin.

Corbin's eyes widened.

"Wait!" I shouted. "He's not infected."

"Daddy?" Sawyer called out, scared.

"I'm not infected. I'm immune," Corbin said. "I can be a cure."

"You concealed a bite mark," masked man said then nodded at the soldier.

Lev stepped forward. "We'll leave. We'll just leave now."

"We can't do that," the man said. "I'm sorry. Laws are laws."

Before we could defend Corbin any further, without any regard to the children in the room, one single shot was fired and Corbin dropped to the ground.

Katie screamed. I clutched her and held her against me. It was the first time I saw my daughter visibly traumatized.

Sawyer raced over to his father's body, crying out over and over for him, kneeling in the blood that pooled around his head.

My heart broke. I wanted to scream and I was shaking uncontrollably.

What did we do? Not only did we lose Billy, but Corbin was dead.

We had to go. There was no way we were staying. Our car was out there, we'd go home.

The man in the mask asked. "Were any of you bitten? We will search you completely."

Before I could respond and say 'don't bother, we're leaving', Katie turned around in my arms.

Sweetly and innocently she said, "My daddy bit me. See?"

She lifted her shirt.

The gun was raised.

Lev leapt forward.

I screamed, "No!"

Bang.

THIRTY

BROKEN

Battered and beaten, we left that camp. Actually, we were taken out. Lev couldn't walk. Had it not been for the kindness of another soldier and the word of a doctor we would have had to leave the camp on foot. Blessedly, they drove us into the line of cars as far as they could and we only had to walk a mile.

We stopped every so many feet and I worried that Lev wouldn't make it through the night. They sent us away without bandages, medical help, nothing.

They told us that we were lucky that Lev wasn't executed because he beat the soldier to within an inch of his life and was the reason for the death of the man in the mask.

I was so panicked when I saw Katie raise her shirt and show her bite mark, so frozen, I could only scream out one long painful, "No!"

Lev reacted.

Before the shot was fired, he sailed shoulder first into the soldier. When I saw that, I grabbed Katie and pulled her back behind me to protect her while reaching for Sawyer.

The gun went off and the bullet hit the man in the mask.

Sawyer scurried to the corner screaming and covering his ears. I placed my hand over Katie's mouth, clutching her so tightly.

Lev pulverized the soldier, fist after fist, punch after punch, like a madman. My mild mannered friend didn't stop until others came into the tent to stop him.

They kicked him and hit him with rifles until Lev didn't move.

They assumed he'd beaten the soldier because of Corbin, and since the man in the mask was dead, no one was left to tell about Katie's bite. We were dragged into the commander's office and the only reason they didn't shoot Lev was because the soldier shot Corbin in front of his son. He understood Lev's enraged reaction and we were freed.

We carried with us the pain of all that. Sawyer was not allowed to come with us so the three of us left alone.

Once we got into the wagon, I drove until I felt we found a safe place to stop for the night.

I didn't know how we were going to face Ben. That radio call to him was the most painful call. He told me how to help Lev and Fleck offered to drive to meet us. But there was nothing Fleck could do. We had to wait until first light to leave.

I cried the entire night, worried about Lev, listening to Katie sob.

My strong, invincible daughter was broken and I couldn't bear it.

Corbin was a good man who didn't deserve what happened. I kept thinking about Sawyer and how he would never be the same again in his life.

I couldn't put it behind me and I never would.

Why did we ever leave the cabin?

Lev drifted in and out of consciousness all night. Each time he fell asleep I didn't think he'd wake up. Like the time Addy had a concussion, I woke him every fifteen minutes.

I did the best I could medically, and drove as fast as I could as soon as it was light.

Ben was waiting and prepared when we arrived. He had to perform surgery on Lev's stomach; he had two broken ribs, although surprisingly the leg was fine. His head injury was the worst part and the reason we couldn't do anything but wait.

He would make it, we all would, but we would never be the same.

EPILOGUE

ONE YEAR LATER

Lev had a long recovery. It took a good month, and he remained weak well into the cooler months. He tried to portray strength, but he wasn't strong. He lost a lot of weight, walked with a limp, and tired easily. His spirits were down and he blamed himself for Corbin's death. Although we tried to convince him otherwise, he wouldn't have it.

Because of his mental state and physical wellbeing, we stayed at the cabin through the winter months.

It was a mild winter with only a few bouts of snow. We had enough wood to stay warm, the well never froze, and deer were plenty. Though we never went hungry or cold, we never forgot those we lost.

During the early months of winter we made radio contact with Hal. He had made it to Canada and left, not because of their staunch rules, but rather the infection had finally hit there. They were battling it like we had.

We fought it first and were done first. The winter proved to be cleansing. In the wake of spring came a certain amount of freshness. Things were green, there was an abundance of birds, and we hadn't seen an infected or dead since fall.

Baby Christian was strong and Bella grew restless, as any teenager would. Katie took as long as Lev to heal emotionally. Sometimes I'd still look at her and see she thought a lot about what she witnessed with Corbin and relived it often. I know I did. With spring in full force, we made a group decision that it was time to leave the cabin. We did so with neither regrets nor any second guessing.

We didn't head north, we headed south. Not to look for life or other groups, but to start anew, go somewhere different.

We set our sights on the Florida Keys and packed everything we could.

Our journey was slow because we stopped a lot, moving at our own pace. We ran into a few survivors here and there who had set up communities. We never stayed, though, we kept moving.

We also never saw another infected. No one had. It was finally over.

The Keys had been colonized and protected by a small faction of survivors and residents who had lived there. They welcomed us.

I wasn't sure how long me, Lev, and Katie would stay; we had a whole big empty world ahead of us that we wanted to explore. One that was no longer dead and was on its way to being alive once again.

For the time being we settled in Florida. Although it was far from home, the painful memories of what happened up north were always with us. They were a part of us. We would carry them with us and build upon them as we started our new life.

All of us, Lev, me, Ben, Bella, Fleck...we lost our families and became a family. Time gave that to us. Time would eventually heal us.

We'd survived a world that fought diligently against us. We weren't better for our struggles, we were merely different. Broken at times and sad, but still alive and together.

In the end, that was what was important.

A message from the author

Thank you so much for reading this book. I hope you enjoyed it. Please visit my website www.jacquelinedruga.com and sign up for my mailing list for updates, freebies, new releases, and giveaways. And don't forget my new Kindle club!

Your support is invaluable to me. I welcome and respond to your feedback.

Please feel free to email me at: Jacqueline@jacquelinedruga.com.